AR Quiz # 49792
BL 3.8
AR Pts 4.0

# THE SUMMER OF
# RILEY

by *Eve Bunting*

JOANNA COTLER BOOKS

*An Imprint of* HarperCollins*Publishers*

Library of Congress Cataloging-in-Publication Data
Bunting, Eve, date.
The summer of Riley / by Eve Bunting.
    p.   cm.
"Joanna Cotler Books."
Summary: Shortly after he gets the perfect dog, Riley, eleven-year-old William must fight for his
dog's life after Riley is taken away because he chases and injures an elderly neighbor's old horse.
ISBN 0-06-029141-9 — ISBN 0-06-029142-7 (lib. bdg.)
    [1. Dogs—Fiction. 2. Divorce—Fiction. 3. Oregon—Fiction.] I. Title.
PZ7.B91527 Stu 2001                                                                     00-63203
[Fic]—dc21

Typography by Alicia Mikles     2 3 4 5 6 7 8 9 10 ❖ First Edition

To the memory of Toby

*Special thanks to Bob Bean, Horse Trainer,*
*and to Carole Peggar.*
*You helped.*

*Chapter 1*

I got my dog, Riley, exactly two months after my grandpa died. Grandpa lived with us and he was my best pal. To tell the truth, I think Mom let me get a dog so I'd start feeling better.

She drove Grace and me into Portland because it's good to get an animal from the pound. You could be saving its life. I picked mine out from all the other dogs right away. A Lab, not quite purebred, but great-looking anyway. His coat was the color of a lion's, but smooth and shiny.

"I'd say he's got some collie in him, too," the pound man told us.

"I thought you wanted a middle-sized dog," Grace said.

"I *thought* I did." I hugged Riley around his middle. "I changed."

Grace nodded. "Cool!"

Grace is my best friend, even if she is a girl. I guess boys, or at least boys my age, which is eleven, are not supposed to even like girls. But I like Grace, and I don't care what anybody thinks.

"Was he a stray?" Mom asked the pound man.

He shook his head. "He was turned in by his owners. That's how come he has a name already." He looked at me. "You can change it if you like."

"Uh-uh," I said. "Riley's just fine."

Mom was frowning. "Why did his owners turn him in? He's not a biter, is he?"

"No way." The pound man put his hand under Riley's chin. "Is this the face of a biter? I can spot one of those right away. They even smell bad tempered."

He rubbed his knuckles up and down on Riley's forehead, and Riley squirmed with joy.

Soon as he stopped rubbing, I started. "I'll do this for you every day when we get home, Riley," I whispered. "Okay?"

"I think his owners had to move and couldn't take him," the pound man told us. "It wasn't that they didn't want him."

"I think we want him. Right, William?" Mom smiled at me.

The pound man looked at Mom. Grace gave me

a nudge. We always think it's funny the way guys about drop dead over Mom.

"He likes her," Grace whispered to me.

"At least he didn't ask her if she's my *sister*," I whispered back.

While we were signing the papers and paying for all the things you have to pay for before you adopt a dog, we told everyone how Riley was going to love being with us, how we were going to take great care of him, and how we have a nice fenced yard that runs all the way round our house for him to play in. The yard's a field, really, since where we live is almost in the country. Grace's house is a half mile or so down the road, toward Monk's Hill where we go to school, and there's only Mrs. Peachwood's little ranch in between.

"Sounds great," the pound man said.

"He wishes *he* was coming with us," Grace whispered.

Riley sat in the back of the station wagon with Grace and me. "You can tell he's really smart," Grace said. "Look at the way he sits up straight and looks out the window. Most dogs would be freaking all over the place."

I patted his head. "I knew he was smart the

minute I saw him." Actually I'd never thought about
his smarts. I just loved his face, his velvety ears, the
way he licked my face with slobbery kisses—the dog
smell of him. I buried my nose in his neck and took
a good sniff now.

Mom grinned at me in the rearview mirror. "I
think it was love at first sight, right, William?"

I rolled my eyes. "Oh, Mom!"

We let Grace off at her driveway because she goes
to her flute lesson on Tuesdays.

"That's Mrs. Peachwood's house," I told Riley, as
we passed our next-door neighbor's. "We usually call
her Peachie. Most of the time she's out in the front
field there with her horse. His name is the Sultan of
Kaboor. You'll like him a lot. Right now the two of
them have gone to Peachie's sister's up in Washing-
ton. They go every July. And over there is our house.
Do you like it, Riley? It's your house too now." And I
felt this great rush of happiness, the kind I hadn't had
since Grandpa died.

But when we turned into our long, dusty driveway,
I couldn't help thinking how great it would have been
if Grandpa had been in the house, waiting for us.
Close by the porch was the big hole he and I'd dug for
the fishpond—and the humongous pile of earth

beside it. We were turning that into a rock garden. The pond was going to be two feet deep and ten by ten feet wide. At first we'd thought it would be round, but we'd decided on free-form instead. It's easier.

We'd already been to Pete's Hardware in Monk's Hill and ordered the pump and filter for the pond. They were supposed to be delivered in two weeks from some place in California. They hadn't come, and it had been two months. Maybe Mom had canceled them, or maybe Pete just knew that fishpond would never be finished and canceled them himself. The big roll of black butyl liner was still rolled up on the porch. There'd been days and nights of rain since Grandpa died, and our hole was a great muddy puddle with dead leaves floating in it. The mound of earth was solid mud.

"William?" Mom had said gently, about a week after Grandpa died. "How about us finishing that pond, you and I?"

"Uh-uh," I'd said, tears swelling up behind my eyes. "Not without Grandpa."

"Well, then, how about filling it in?" she'd asked me twice. "We can't just leave it," she'd begged. The second time she'd said, "We could call Dad. He'd help you. The two of you could work together."

For a minute I'd been tempted. I had high hopes that one day Dad would come back and decide to stay. And it would take time for us to fill in the pond and even more if we decided to finish it. Lots of things could happen. But in the end I knew I didn't want anybody, even Dad, working on the pond that was Grandpa's and mine.

The tears had spilled over just thinking about it, and Mom had hugged me against her and said, "Okay. Let's not talk about it anymore for now."

And we didn't.

It was funny about the fishpond. While it lay there, waiting, it was as if Grandpa would come back and I'd see him standing in it, his glasses all muddy, his baseball cap so dirty you could hardly see what color it was. And he'd be shouting, "Come on, William. No slacking. We got work to do."

I blinked. He wasn't there leaning on his spade, waiting for me. Not today.

I opened the door of the station wagon, and Riley scrambled over my legs and bounded out. He raced round and round the yard, making his own path through the long grass. He dashed through the rhododendron bushes, knocking off some of the big flowers, stopped to spray the trunk of every single pine tree, then rushed toward the hole. He paused at its edge and looked back at me. Did he understand?

"He *is* smart," Mom said. "A lot of dogs would just have jumped in there and wallowed in all that mud. Then what a mess we would have had." She spoke uncertainly, the way she does now every time she mentions the pond.

"Let's take a few pictures," she said. "Stand close to Riley." She took lots of him and me, and me and him, and I swear that dog stood absolutely still and just about smiled for the camera.

"I think Riley is the perfect dog," I said.

And that's what I thought, then.

# Chapter 2

I showed Riley our house. He walked sedately around with me, checking out the furniture, getting acquainted. He didn't try to pee anywhere, and I thought that was a good sign of his house manners.

Afterward, I took him outside. Our yard was filled with late afternoon sunshine. Hundreds of gnat-catchers twittered through the air. In the far distance I could see the mountains. Once Dad took me hiking up there and we saw a humongous bear. Fortunately, it didn't see us.

Riley and I played Frisbee and catch and running games all afternoon. When Mom told us to come in for dinner, he stayed beside me on the braided rug and didn't even whine for food.

"Somebody taught that dog to be polite," Mom said.

Grace called at about seven for a report. I told her

Riley was the best dog ever.

"Can he sit up and beg?" she asked.

"Give me a break," I said. "This dog has dignity. This dog doesn't beg."

Later I called Dad and left a message on his answering machine. "I got a dog today," I told him. "Can you come see him?"

I put the receiver back real quietly, and I tried not to wonder where Dad was. It was 9:30. I always try not to wonder where he is when I call at night and he isn't home. There's a commercial, I guess it's a commercial, on TV where this guy says, "It's after midnight. Do you know where your children are?" Change that to "your dad." Of course, it wasn't after midnight yet. And he was probably still at work. I was sure that's where he was.

Riley slept with me, warm and solid, his big head taking up most of my pillow.

"Just this one night," Mom told us both. "So he'll feel welcome."

"Sure, just this one night," I repeated, and I winked at Riley. I thought he winked back.

When she put out the light, we talked. I tell you, if you were a scaredy-baby kind of kid, you'd never be scared if you had Riley in bed with you. He could fend off monsters or robbers or anything else that happened to drop by. I explained to him about Dad.

"They used to get along great, he and Mom," I whispered, my mouth close to his ear. "I can't figure why they didn't try harder to stay together. I mean, he has this rented house over in Cave Junction now, and we live here. It's nuts if you ask me. Mom says there are things between them that can't be fixed and they're happier apart. But what about me? Am I supposed to be happier without a dad?" I could tell Riley was listening. "And then there's Grandpa," I said, blinking away tears. "I miss him a lot," I said. "A lot," I repeated.

Riley snuggled closer.

I found the place on his forehead between his eyes and gave him a knuckle rub.

Grace came over the next day and we took Riley on a run. That was the beginning of the things we all did together. He went swimming with us in Chiltern Dam, his head slick and smooth as a seal's above the water. Sometimes we hitched my skateboard to him and he pulled us each in turn.

"I wish I had a dog instead of two brothers," Grace said.

My grandpa had bad allergies. That's why we couldn't have a dog before. But I'd rather have a grandpa, even though I loved Riley already.

Sometimes I took Riley out by myself. Once a little bitsy rat of a dog came pattering right over to us and I was nervous.

The little dog wasn't on a leash and Riley could have swallowed him in one bite.

"Be good, Riley," I whispered, holding tight to his collar.

But Riley just nuzzled the little guy, friendly as could be.

"What a nice dog," the lady owner said, panting to a stop beside us. I could tell she was as nervous as I'd been.

"He is," I said.

One morning Riley and I went on a whole day hike. Mom wasn't up yet so we left her a note.

I fixed myself a thick peanut butter and applesauce sandwich. It tastes great when the applesauce has time to soak into the bread so that it's nice and mooshy. Then I tipped a bowlful of kibble into a bag and added four dog biscuits for Riley. "A pooch gets hungry in the great out-of-doors," I told him.

Dad had given me a compass once and explained about the magnetic north. I showed it to Riley before I slipped it in my pocket. "In case we get lost," I said. "Though I don't know how that could happen since I've been in the river woods a jillion times."

We set off. A boy and his dog go hiking, I thought, and I felt like Tom Sawyer or Huckleberry Finn off on an adventure.

As soon as we got on the river path, I let Riley off his leash. Heck, no sweat if we met another dog. Riley would be cool with it. We'd been through that already.

He romped ahead of me, snuffling at gopher holes, barking at things up trees that I couldn't even see, rushing down every now and then to lap up river water in great noisy gulps.

"Don't fall in," I warned him and he laughed back at me, as if to say, "What do you think I am, a dodo?"

And then it turned out that I was the one who fell in. Actually I just slipped and slithered on my rear end, bumping and banging against rocks, ending up ankle-deep in the water.

Riley scrambled after me, grabbing my wrist in his teeth and tugging fiercely.

"Hey! Hey! It's all right," I told him, pulling each

foot out of the sucking mud. "Let go of me, Riley. I'm not drowning here. Give me a break. Look, I'm out already."

But he held on, bracing his legs and dragging me away from the river's edge.

"Okay, pal," I said. I looked back at where I'd been standing and saw that just beyond that, maybe six inches from where I'd stood, the river dropped off into a deep, dark hole. Another step and I'd have been in it, up to my shoulders, or even deeper, over my head.

I wrapped my arms around Riley and he licked my face all over with his warm, rough tongue.

What exactly had happened? Had he saved me? Not exactly. I can swim. I could have pulled myself out. Had he sensed I was in danger? Was he scared for me? Was he trying to protect me?

"Thanks, puppy," I whispered, my face against his neck, and I had this sudden sureness that Riley would always be beside me, ready to help me if I needed help. "You're my dog," I whispered. "And you know something? If you need help, you'll get it from me. Deal?"

Riley wagged his tail.

"Deal," I said. "Now how about lunch?"

∞

That night in bed I thought about Grandpa, and it seemed that thinking didn't hurt as much as it did before. People said time made a difference. That you felt better as the days went on. But I hadn't felt better. Riley was lying next to me, snoring softly. I stroked his head.

The next day I tried explaining some of this to Grace without sounding too goofy. Grace understands about me and Grandpa, so I figured she'd probably understand this.

"Maybe that's one of the reasons people get dogs, to kind of close up the empty places inside them," Grace said.

Sometimes Grace is very smart.

# Chapter 3

Grace went home at four because she had to go shopping with her mom.

Riley and I went back up to my room to read and listen to music and shoot the bull. I liked talking to Riley, and even though he didn't answer in words, he said things just by the way he looked at me.

I lay on my bed, watching the sun shadows on my ceiling, my arm around Riley's neck. Mom was fixing lasagna, probably Stouffer's, small size, serves two. The good spicy smell wafted into my room.

I gave Riley a bite of my cracker. "The thing is," I told him, "just thinking about Dad makes me mad. Sometimes. I mean, I called him and left a message about you, and he never even called back. Or came."

Riley watched me carefully, then nodded.

"I'm—" I began.

There was the sound of a car turning into our driveway.

I jumped up and ran to the window.

"Speak of the Devil," I muttered, and then, so Riley wouldn't get the wrong idea, added, "Not that Dad's a devil. That's just a saying. Anyway, he's here."

I watched his car pull up to the front door and stop. He'd left the gate open. Of course he didn't remember we had a dog now, and a dog had to be kept in. Fortunately, Riley was safe here, with me.

The screen door squeaked open and I heard Mom's and Dad's voices in the kitchen.

I was about to grab Riley and rush down the stairs, but then I decided to be cautious. With Mom and Dad, it's better to scope things out first.

"Be very quiet," I warned Riley, and grabbed his collar.

Together we padded to the bend in the stairs. You can't see into the kitchen from there, and whoever is in the kitchen can't see you. But you can hear. It's bad to eavesdrop. It's sneaky and rotten and sometimes you hear horrible things about yourself, which I guess serves you right. But sometimes it's the only way to find things out. This was where I was when I first found out Dad was leaving. Then I'd rushed upstairs and crawled under my bed.

"I know it's a long way and you're busy," Mom was saying to Dad in the kitchen. She had this cold, tight voice. "But getting the dog was a big deal to William. He wanted you to be interested. He's been waiting for you to call. We've both left you messages."

Beside me, Riley yawned a big yawn that might have been noisy if I hadn't clapped my hand over his mouth. "Shhh!"

"I *meant* to call," Dad said. "I was up in Seattle at a store managers' meeting for five days and I just forgot. The dog's a collie, right? Is that what you said?"

"He's a Lab mix. Maybe part collie."

Lasagna smells drifted around us. That small-sized lasagna would certainly not be enough if Dad planned on staying.

"Do you want coffee?" Mom asked.

"Sure." Dad sounded relieved. Things were easing up for him.

"So how is Phoebe?" Mom asked politely.

"She's fine, thank you," he said politely back to her.

I imagined him sitting at the table, long legs crossed at the ankles. Dad's very elegant, or so Grace says.

I took hold of one of Riley's big soft paws and squeezed, but not too hard. Phoebe? Who was Phoebe? Somehow I didn't think she was a dog Dad had gotten for himself for company. All those night-time phone calls when I never could reach him flashed through my head. Phoebe? She sounded like a disease!

"So, don't you think it's about time William was told about her?" Mom asked. "I mean, after an engagement comes a marriage, far as I can re-member."

Nothing but silence and the sound of my own breathing.

He was engaged to the disease.

"Not to change the subject," Dad said, "but when are you going to get that hole outside filled in? It's a mess."

"I'll talk to William again," Mom said, and there was a tremendous clatter of dishes as if she was bang-ing them from the cupboard onto the table.

"Not that what we do is any of your business any-more." She was mimicking the way Dad had said, "Not to change the subject."

This I didn't want to hear. This was a private con-versation and it made me cringe inside.

It reminded me of the way they'd talked to each other back when they lived together, not privately at all, but out loud. No use me thinking, hoping, Dad would ever come back. And now with this awful, horrible Phoebe. . . . I took Riley's collar and the two of us slithered back to my room.

I closed the door silently behind us. I was sweating, so I pulled off my T-shirt and used it to dry my chest and stomach. "Brother!" I said out loud. "How can he even think about getting engaged after being married to Mom?"

"How can he be?" Grace asked, when I called and told her.

"Maybe he'll change his mind," she said.

I wasn't too hopeful.

Chapter 4

On the last day of July, Grace came bursting into our kitchen. "Peachie's back," she said.

I polished off my cereal. "Let's go show her Riley."

"She'll be *enraptured* with him," Grace said. Grace loves important words.

We clipped on Riley's leash and rode down the driveway, gravel scrunching and sparking beneath our bike wheels.

"I wonder what she'll think when she hears about Phoebe," I said.

"Maybe she knows already," Grace said. "Your mom could have called her."

"I guess Mom and I are going to have to meet Phoebe sometime," I said. "That's going to be the all-time worst." Thinking about it took away some of my good feelings about the day.

We rode on in silence.

Peachie was out, twisting wire around the top railing of her gate. We reeled in and braked to a stop.

Over at the far end of the field, the Sultan of Kaboor was peacefully cropping the grass, which was studded with white clover, thick as snowflakes. I thought it was a beautiful picture, the kind you'd see in a calendar. The mountains in the distance looked almost fake.

"How's the Sultan?" Grace asked. "Did he have a good vacation?"

"Yep. We both did." Peachie leaned over the gate to stroke Riley's head. "So you got your dog, William! He's a beaut!"

"Thanks," I began, pleased that Peachie was enraptured and hadn't mentioned Phoebe. "I wanted him to meet—" and then it was like a volcano erupting next to me. Riley jerked on the leash, tearing the red handle out of my grip, dashing like a mad creature around the fence.

On the other side of the field, the Sultan had broken into a stately old horse trot, paying no attention to us or to the big yellow dog that was hurtling in his direction. The jerk on the leash had pulled me right off my bike, and it and I were sprawled on the dirt in front of Peachie's gate.

Grace was screaming, "Riley! Riley! Come back here," but Riley seemed beyond hearing.

"Riley!" I yelled. "You come back . . ."

He leaped the fence. Thinking about it afterward, it seemed as if he cleared that fence the way a high jumper clears a hurdle, with air between him and the top railing. His leash trailed behind him, caught for a second, then freed up. I was still on my stomach, paralyzed.

Peachie was shouting, too. "Don't you dare! Don't you touch that horse!"

The Sultan, who probably doesn't hear all that well anymore, suddenly did hear, or sense, the whirl-wind that was launching itself at him. He tried to run. Once, the Sultan of Kaboor had been a great racehorse. He'd won more than fifty races here in Oregon. He'd won the Long Acres Miles back in the eighties, before I was even born. He'd sired champion fillies and colts, but all that was long ago. Now he was just an old, almost blind, almost deaf horse. Peachie was running toward him as fast as she could, but she's old, too. Her straw hat flew off. Her red shirt puffed up around her.

Grace scrambled over the gate with me right

behind her and then we both stopped in horror. One minute Riley was snapping at the Sultan's heels and the Sultan was whinnying and kicking back. The next minute the Sultan was down.

Peachie had reached them. She pounded on Riley with her hands, big in her work gloves. "Get away from him," she screamed. "Git! Git!"

Riley began backing away. I grabbed the red leash handle. "What did you do that for?" I groaned. Beyond him I could see the Sultan, lying there, Peachie on her knees beside him. I don't know about Grace, but I was scared out of my wits.

"Bad dog! Bad dog!" I whispered, but the words sounded wimpy and stupid and not nearly strong enough. I didn't know whether to go across to Peachie and the Sultan or run for home.

Grace raced past me. "Oh, Sultan, poor Sultan," she sobbed. Grace loves the Sultan. She visits him all the time and brings him carrots and apples. She was crying hard now.

I walked slowly behind her, Riley beside me, reeled in tight. He had a slinky look to him, and even though he was walking, he was pulling back. I knew he knew what he'd done was unforgivable. He knew all right.

Peachie had the Sultan's head in her lap. There was foam on his mouth and Grace was wiping it off with one of Peachie's gloves.

"I'm sorry, Peachie," I began.

"Don't you bring that dog anywhere near my horse," Peachie said over her shoulder. I'd never heard nice Peachie so filled with rage. "Get him out of here."

"But . . . is the Sultan going to be all right? Can I—"

"Go away. Take that dog out of my sight."

I backed off.

Neither Peachie, nor Grace, nor the Sultan watched us go.

"What did you do that for?" I whispered fiercely to Riley. "That was bad, bad, bad." I shook the leash every time I said "bad," jerking on his neck.

Riley stared up at me, squinchy eyed.

"You're going to be in trouble," I told him. "Big, big trouble."

# Chapter 5

I blurted out what had happened the minute I got through the kitchen door.

Mom sank into a chair and put her hands over her mouth.

I unclipped Riley's leash, and he dropped down onto the braided rug and closed his eyes.

"How awful," Mom said. "Poor Sultan. Poor Peachie. I have to go over there. But what am I going to say to her? That horse is her life. Did she call Doctor Webb?"

Dr. Webb is our local vet.

"I don't know."

Mom stood and paced from the window to the front door and back, staring in the direction of Peachie's house, which you can't really see from here, across the fence and through the trees. You can see it from my bedroom, but at least she didn't go up there to look. She pulled a square of paper towel, wiped her eyes, then pulled another square for me.

"Where's Grace?" She peered around the kitchen, as if Grace was there and she hadn't noticed her.

"She . . ."

And just then, Grace arrived.

We stared at her, afraid to ask. I took a deep breath. "Well? How is he? Is he okay?"

"He was able to get up. Doc Webb's on his way. I called him from Peachie's." Grace touched Riley with the toe of her Nike. "How could you do that to the Sultan of Kaboor, dog? How could you?"

Riley opened his eyes and closed them again.

"Don't kick him," I said sharply. "He didn't know."

"I'm not kicking him. But I'd like to," Grace said.

"William, you and I've got to go over there right now," Mom said. "Grace, will you stay till we come back? And will you make sure Riley doesn't get out?"

Grace nodded and gave me an angry look.

I didn't want to go to Peachie's. What if the Sultan had a broken leg or something? Well, he couldn't have. Grace said he had gotten up. He could have hurt something else, though. Something inside of him.

But I had to go.

❧   ❧   ❧

Peachie stood next to the Sultan in the field. He was up, but I could see his skinny old legs shaking.

"Is he . . . is he okay?" Mom put her hand on Peachie's shoulder. "I can't tell you how sorry we are."

Peachie's voice was so low I could hardly hear her. She didn't turn to face us, just stood there stroking the Sultan's neck.

"I was remembering the day he raced for us at Del Mar. He was so beautiful, his mane flying, the jockey low on his neck. Brad Falcon was riding him that day. Del Mar is so beautiful. All that green, green grass." Her voice was dreamy. "The air so soft. The palm trees. And the whole stand alive with people on their feet, shouting his name. It was like thunder. 'Sultan! Sultan of Kaboor!' And Woodie just beside himself."

Woodie was Mr. Peachwood, Peachie's husband. I never knew him. I guess he died before I was even born. Peachie and Woodie.

"Woodie loved the Sultan." Still that dreamy voice. "You can have twenty, thirty horses in your lifetime, but there's always one that's special. Like your first love."

The Sultan of Kaboor stood blinking as if the light hurt his poor old eyes, while Peachie's hand soothed his neck, soothed and soothed.

I swallowed hard. This was even worse than I'd imagined.

"He deserves a peaceful old age," Peachie said, turning to look at us for the first time. "And I'm going to see that he gets it. This can never happen again. Never."

"No," Mom said in a choky sort of way. "It never will. I promise you, Peachie."

"I'd like you to go now," Peachie told us. Our Peachie. This stranger with the cold, cold face. Our dear old friend. She sounded as if she hated us. Probably she did.

We met Doc Webb hurrying through the gate.

"Bad business," he said. "Whose dog was it, anyway?"

"Ours," Mom said grimly, and marched grimly on.

We had a meeting around the kitchen table, Mom and Grace and I. Riley was a silent partner, not at the table but under it.

"So, what are we going to do, William?" Mom asked.

"Well, I'll hold him real tight when we're out. The thing was, I wasn't expecting him to do what he did. I'll be on my guard now. He won't get away from me."

"He's a big, strong dog," Mom said.

"I'll . . . I'll never take him past Peachie's yard."

Mom shook her head. "That would be impossible, William. If we take him out of the yard at all, we're going to pass Peachie's. You mean you'll never take him down to the river? Or into the trees?"

"I won't; I don't have to. I can go the other way."

"You won't stick with that," Grace said. "You should make a rule right now to never let that dog out of your yard." Grace's eyes were puffy from crying and she kept getting up to see if Doc's truck was still there, or if she could catch a glimpse of the Sultan, and then she'd look down at Riley with that mean, unforgiving look.

"But why did he do it?" Mom asked. "I keep coming back to that."

"I think it was a onetime thing," I said quickly. "You know, he just got this idea in his head. Maybe the Sultan reminded him of a horse he knew once that he didn't like. I bet he never does it again."

It was Grace who spotted Doc Webb crossing Peachie's field on his way to his truck. She and Mom and I ran out to catch him before he left, and the most awful thing happened. Riley bounded out behind me, but I didn't see him until Grace shouted, "Riley!" I had to grab his collar and trail him back in.

"See?" Grace said.

"I—I'm just not used to having to be careful yet," I stammered. "He won't get past me next time."

There was that furious Grace-look again.

We surrounded Doc Webb.

"He's real shaken up," the Doc said. "Far as I can tell, nothing's broken, but he's hurting and he has a ruptured tendon on the right foreleg. He's resting in the barn." He opened the door of his truck and threw his black bag on the passenger seat. "Trouble is, with an old horse like that, you can't take chances. If this happens again, it could be real bad."

Mom slumped against the truck. "I can't believe this happened."

"I've left Peachie a tranquilizer for him," the Doc said. "And I've wrapped his leg with a support bandage. I'll be keeping an eye on him."

We watched him drive away.

Back in the kitchen, we took up our conversation where we'd left off.

"I've got a bad feeling," Mom said. "Do you think

this could be why the last owners took Riley to the pound?"

"It was so vicious the way he—" Grace began.

I slapped my fist on the table. "Give it a rest, Grace. We've been over all that."

"William! Don't you talk to Grace like that!" Mom said.

Grace pushed her chair back. "You know what, William? I like Riley a lot. But I like the Sultan, too."

"You're not very loyal," I began. "Riley didn't—"

"He was horrible to the Sultan. Just admit it, William." The screen door banged behind her and she was gone.

Mom reached over and took my hand. "I called Dad," she said. "I left him a message about . . . what happened."

"Good luck," I muttered.

Mom's eyes were soft. "You know something, sweetheart? Maybe Riley isn't the dog for us. If we took him back, we could get you another dog." She smiled a fake smile. "A middle-sized dog. The kind you wanted in the first place."

I wriggled my hand out of hers.

"It's just too big a chance to take," she went on.

"What if Riley gets to poor old Sultan again? And what if next time Sultan doesn't make it? How will we feel then?"

"It won't happen," I said. "It won't. It won't."

# Chapter 6

The day seemed longer by far than a normal day. I kept waiting for something, I didn't know what. It would have been nice if Grace had called to say she was sorry for being so mean about Riley, but she didn't. She was probably sitting at her computer not even thinking about me or Riley. Well, I wouldn't think about her either, except some bad thoughts.

After lunch, Mom baked brownies for Peachie from one of her mixes. Mom has boxes and packages for everything. Even I can make Rice-a-Roni, the San Francisco treat, or Tuna Dinner, nothing to add but the tuna. She says she's a hopeless cook, but I don't know. Everything tastes great.

"I hope Peachie opens the door to me," Mom said grimly, as she marched off.

I took Riley out in the yard, and for the first time

I kept his leash on. It was too easy to remember the way he had jumped over Peachie's fence with all those inches to spare. He kept looking at me as if he couldn't understand why he wasn't as free as a bird, and I kept telling him, "It's because you did that bad thing to the Sultan. You have to earn our trust again." Maybe some of it went into his dog brain.

When Mom came back, she said she thought Peachie liked the brownies, and they'd taken one out to the Sultan, who definitely had not lost his appetite. She said that actually Peachie looked more shaken up than the Sultan did.

I took my dog and my comic books and went upstairs to lie on my bed and listen to my stereo. I turned the volume up really loud. Usually listening to my CDs takes my mind off my troubles. But today it didn't. My thoughts wouldn't let go. If I couldn't take Riley out into the yard and let him run free, then he'd have to be tied up. I went to the window and looked down. If we tied him to the porch rail, he could get shade if it was hot and shelter when it rained. With a long rope, he could go in a sort of semicircle down to the gate. But it would still be awful for him. Awful. Cruel to chain a dog up like that. I wanted to cry.

From here I could see over the slant of our back porch roof. I stared down into Peachie's yard. There was the barn with its half door closed. The Sultan would be inside, being careful not to put his weight on his poor sore leg. "Bad dog," I told Riley, and then hugged him hard because I felt so sorry for him, too, sorry for all of us. "Stay!" I told him. I closed him in and went down the corridor to Grandpa's room.

As soon as I opened the door, my heart began to pump. My chest was suffocating me. I sat on the edge of Grandpa's bed and looked down at my feet in my dirty socks. It was so stuffy in here. Stuffy, as if the room had died, too. "Grandpa," I whispered. "I miss you. If you were here, you'd help. You always gave me good advice."

I was still sitting there when I heard Dad's car in the driveway. I know the sound of his car by heart. Twice in one week, I thought. We're honored. And then I thought, what if he's brought horrible Phoebe, and I ran to the window. He was by himself.

I left Riley closed up in my room and went to my eavesdropping corner of the stairs.

"So, what is this big problem he's had with the dog?" Dad asked Mom.

I listened as she told him.

"Humm!" Dad was considering. I imagined him sitting at the table, head tilted, that interested look on his face. Dad could really pay attention when he wanted to. "Well, the dog has to go back," he said at last. "You don't want a lawsuit. And believe me, Peachie may be a good friend, but she's not going to put up with this sort of thing."

"I know. We could try obedience training or . . ." Mom paused. "Is there such a thing as a dog psychiatrist?" Mom asked. "I'd pay for it. I wouldn't care. William already loves this dog so much. You know, with his grandpa dying . . . that was such a blow for him. And then not having you around. . . ."

"Give me a break, Dorothy." I could feel his anger. "It's been three years."

I slithered back to my room.

Riley wagged his tail, happy to see me.

My window was closed, and I opened it and leaned out, letting the nice cool air fan my skin. The sun was going down and the sky was striped pink. When it looks like that, it reminds me of streaky bacon, only prettier. The Sultan's head was poking out over the half door of his barn, and I waved to him to show how friendly I was. Riley came and put his paws on the windowsill beside me.

"I expect Dad will come up here any minute," I said. "Probably he won't tell us about Phoebe today because . . . Well, in the first place he's probably chicken, and then there's the problem with you. 'Problem!' That's what he called it. More like a . . . prank. Yeah, you were having fun and it changed into something else. I'll explain."

I turned to look at Riley, to check that he was listening, and suddenly there was this frantic scramble beside me, the force of a big body shoving me to the side, back claws scraping on my windowsill, a jump and he was on the roof of the back porch, another jump and he was off the roof and onto the gravel driveway.

"Riley!" I screamed. "NO!" Because I knew right away where he was headed. "Peachie!" I screamed. "Help!"

I saw him jump the fence, fly over it, and I rushed for my door, half falling down the stairs, screaming, "Mom! Mom! Riley's out!"

Their shocked faces shimmered in front of me, and then I was running past them, hearing them behind me. I couldn't jump the fence, no way. I raced like mad down the driveway, through the open gate, hearing the Sultan's loud, terrified whinny, remembering that half door to the barn. Riley could clear it easily. Now I was at Peachie's gate, Mom and Dad at my heels, and I stopped.

Peachie stood in front of the barn door, her arms outstretched, and Riley was crouched in front of her, not threatening at all, kind of friendly looking, his tail wagging, watching her.

"Go home!" Peachie screamed. "Get away!"

But Riley still stood, hopeful, as if waiting for a treat. I ran as fast as I could and grabbed his collar, and Mom was saying, "Oh, Peachie, are you all right? Oh, Peachie!" and Dad was shouting at Riley, "Scat! Scat! William! Get him out of here."

I had his collar. He didn't want to come, but I tugged him away. His paws took him forward with me, but his head kept turning back.

I pulled him into the house and back up to my room, closed the window and bolted it, then closed the bedroom door. It was about five minutes before Mom and Dad came back, Dad with his arm around Mom's shoulders and her leaning against him, which is a sight that would have cheered me at any other time.

"Sit down, Dorothy," Dad said gently. "I'll make you some tea. Do you still take sugar? Do you still keep it in the same place?"

The kitchen was filled with the nasty smell of burning lasagna.

"Mom?" I said. "Riley was trying to be friendly. He's not out to get the Sultan. He likes him. Don't you see? He was wagging his tail."

We watched in silence as Dad made the tea—heated the pot, got out the good china cups with the forget-me-nots on them, put the tea cozy on the pot.

"Have to let it draw, right?" he asked Mom with a faint smile. "I remember."

"You were the one who taught me," Mom said in a tight, teary voice.

The doorbell rang.

"Oh, no!" Mom said, all panicky. "It's Peachie."

"It's not," Dad said. "It's okay, Dorothy. Peachie's not going to come over here. Relax."

"Maybe it's Grace," I said, like Grace ever comes to the front door or rings the bell.

Dad smoothed his hair and went to open the door.

He was right. It wasn't Peachie. And it wasn't Grace either.

# Chapter 7

I looked past Dad to the man and woman standing on the porch. They were in uniform—brown pants and lighter brown shirts. I knew the woman, and I felt like reaching out and slamming the door so the two of them couldn't get in. The woman's name was Mrs. Zemach, Officer Zemach, I guess. Her daughter Yvonne goes to our school. Grace says Yvonne picks her nose, but I've never seen her do it. Officer Zemach came to school to speak to us on Career Day. She wore the same uniform then. Mrs. Zemach is an animal-control officer.

She saw me and said, "Hello, William."

"Hi." I glanced past her to the truck, the kind with the mesh in back, parked in our driveway.

"I'm Officer Dobbs and this is Officer Zemach," the man said. "We're from animal control. May we come in?"

"Please." Dad moved aside.

They stepped into the living room.

"Thanks." They followed Mom and Dad to the kitchen, and I trailed behind.

"How's it going, young man?" Officer Dobbs asked over his shoulder.

"Fine," I muttered, which is what you say even when things are as bad as they can possibly be. Like now.

As soon as we went into the kitchen, Officer Zemach said, "Uh-oh, something's burning." But Mom didn't seem to hear.

Dad took two extra cups from the cupboard.

"I suppose it's about the dog?" he asked, and Officer Dobbs nodded.

"'Fraid so." He jerked his head in the direction of Peachie's house, as if Dad might not know exactly what he was talking about. "Mrs. Peachwood has lodged a complaint. Seems like your dog's been after her horse." He stroked his skinny little mustache with one finger.

"My word," Dad said. "She didn't waste much time."

"We happened to be in Monk's Hill when we got the call." Officer Dobbs sounded apologetic for getting here so fast.

"Do you want to check that oven, Mrs. Halston?" Officer Zemach said in a low voice to Mom. "Smells like the whole house could go up in flames any minute."

Mom walked across the kitchen and turned the knob on the oven, but she didn't take out whatever was in there.

"What exactly is it you want us to do about the dog?" Dad asked. "The Humane Society people should have told my son about this problem before they sold it to him." He sounded very aristocratic.

"Probably they didn't know," Officer Zemach said mildly.

"We thought he was the perfect dog," Mom whispered.

Upstairs Riley whined and scratched at my bedroom door.

Officer Dobbs stroked his mustache some more. "It's not what we *want* to do about the dog, Mr. Halston. It's what we have to do after that kind of complaint." He put his hand on my shoulder. "I'm sorry, son. You haven't had him that long, have you?"

"Long enough," I muttered.

"That's just as well," he said.

That suffocating feeling was in my chest again, as

if somebody were sitting on me, squeezing my air out.

"We have to take him," the officer said.

I wet my lips. "Where?"

"Back to Portland. To the animal shelter."

"You mean, return him?" It sounded like Christmas when you get something too big or too small or too disgusting and you have to take it back for an exchange. But I didn't want an exchange.

"That's right. Return him."

It was Dad who asked the next question. I guess it's always better to know. That's what they say, but I'm never sure. I might have been able to imagine Riley there, being taken care of, given to somebody who lived far away from horses, maybe somebody in Portland, right in the middle of the city. "What will they do with him?" Dad asked.

"Well." The two officers exchanged glances. "We'll have to wait and see. There's a law, you know. I'm afraid he might have to be put to sleep."

"*Killed.*" The word blasted out of me. "No! You don't mean that!"

Officer Zemach's eyes were kind. "I'm sorry, William. A dog that chases livestock in this state—well, he has to be destroyed. That's the law, and there's no getting away from it."

"We were planning on taking him to obedience school or finding a dog psychiatrist," Mom said faintly. "Couldn't we give that a try? We could watch him every minute and then see if dog classes or a psychiatrist could help him. He's such a nice dog in every other way."

The two officers looked at each other. "I'm afraid we have to take him right now."

All kinds of thoughts jumped through my head. No way. I wouldn't let them take him. He was my dog. I'd stand in front of my door the way Peachie had stood in front of the barn. Or I'd go right now, and pretend to get him and we'd both jump out of the window, drop onto the roof. We'd run. We'd hide. Grace would help us. She liked Riley even if she was mad at him. She wouldn't want him killed.

"I'll get him," Dad said. "I don't want my son to have to bring him down. Where's his leash, William?"

"No place!" I shouted.

"It's by the door," Mom said in a defeated kind of way.

"You can't have him," I told Dad. "You don't even know him. He's mine. I'm—"

"William," Dad said. "There's no argument about this. I wish there were."

I blocked the bottom of the stairs. "You're not my dad anymore. You can't tell me what to do."

"Move, son. The dog has to go."

He pushed past me and I went up after him, dragging on the back of his shirt. "Please, Dad. Please, no."

He opened the bedroom door and Riley came bounding out, crazy with joy, rushing past Dad to me, almost knocking me backward down the stairs, he was so happy to see me.

I grabbed him around the neck and tried not to let Dad clip the leash onto his collar. "No. No." I kept pushing his hand away.

"Stop it, William." Dad was angry now.

Officer Dobbs was coming up the stairs with Mom behind him. "Easy, son," he said. "Easy."

"Doesn't he even get a trial?" I shouted. "This is supposed to be America."

I rushed into my room, banged the door, locked it, and crawled under my bed. I was crying in big, noisy gulps.

Even though I put my hands over my ears, I heard Riley whine. I heard the doors of the truck slam, heard the wheels crunch down the driveway. I didn't hear our creaky gate close. They'd left it open. Well, we didn't need to worry about that anymore.

# Chapter 8

Mom came up and knocked on my door. "Come down, sweetie, and eat with us," she called. "Dad has to go pretty soon."

When she came up the second time, I called, "Okay. Okay. I'm coming."

I put a clean T-shirt on and went down.

Mom had fixed a salad and macaroni and cheese, the expensive kind you fix in the oven that has real Parmesan in the package.

Dad sat in the chair that used to be his and I sat in mine. I tried not to think of Riley not being on the rug beside me. I let my arm droop down. That's what I did when he was there, and he'd lick my hand and lick and lick.

I swallowed and pushed my plate away.

"I'm wondering," Mom said. "Could we appeal? Legally, I mean. Should we get a lawyer?"

I sat straight up. "Appeal? That's a great idea."

"After all," Mom said, "Riley didn't bite the Sultan. Surely he doesn't have to be put to sleep for that. Shouldn't it be only if he attacks?"

I nodded hard. "And he didn't attack. We should definitely appeal."

Dad wasn't eating much either. Maybe he'd meant it when he said he was sorry. Or maybe Phoebe's some great cook and he doesn't like Mom's kind of macaroni and cheese anymore.

"The law in Oregon says chasing is enough," he said.

"But that's unfair. That's a rotten unfair law." I tried to hold it back, but a big sob just burped right out of me.

Mom touched my glass. "At least drink your milk, William," she said gently.

I took a sip. "What if Peachie took back her complaint? What if she's sorry now?" I crumpled my napkin and stood up. "I bet she is. Wouldn't it be a good idea if I went over and talked to her? If she took away her complaint, they'd probably let him come home."

"I don't know," Mom said. "But it's worth a try."

"Do you want us to come with you?" Dad asked. "It won't be easy, you know, William. She must have been awfully angry to call the animal-control people. And she probably still is."

"I'll go myself," I said. "Riley's my dog. I'm the one who let him get away."

I ran upstairs to get my shoes, which I'd kicked off. There was that awful window. If only I hadn't opened it.

It was while I was tying my laces that I had a great idea. I opened my keeper box and took out my most recent bank statement, the kind I get once a month. I've been putting birthday money and chore money in the Monk's Hill Savings and Loan for ages, and the statement said I had $348.75. What if . . . ?

I folded the statement small and put it in the pocket of my jeans.

At the bend of the stairs I slowed, then stopped as I heard the angry voices.

"Just think it through," Dad was saying in that unfriendly way he has sometimes with Mom. I've noticed Dad and Mom talk to each other nicer when I'm around. It's a kind of playacting. But when it's just them, it's totally different.

"You shouldn't be encouraging him on this," Dad was saying. "An appeal isn't going to work. And even if it did, what then? You'd get the dog and you'd have

the same problem all over again. This is just something William has to accept."

"He's had to accept too much lately," Mom said.
"And hope is good."

"Not false hope," Dad said in his snooty way.

I heard her draw in a deep breath. "No, not false
hope. I've had plenty of that myself."

I knew she was talking about Dad at the beginning, and how she'd hoped they'd get back together.

And now, with Phoebe, I guess neither of us even
had false hope.

"How long do you think they'll keep the dog
before . . . ?" Mom was asking Dad.

"Five days," Dad said. "I asked them."

I held tight to the banister. Five days! I had to get
Peachie to stop this.

I called her first from Mom's bedroom phone so
they wouldn't hear.

"Peachie? This is William. May I come over and
talk to you?"

There was a pause on the other end. I could hear
*Jeopardy* on her TV. "If you're coming to ask me to
drop those charges, William, you're wasting your
time. I'm sorry. I did what I had to do."

"May I come anyway?"

Another pause.

"They broke Roger Maris's record for the most home runs in a single season," the *Jeopardy* guy was saying.

I knew the question. Peachie would, too. She loves baseball.

The silence stretched and stretched.

"All right," she said at last. "But don't expect too much of me."

"I won't." Which, of course, was a lie.

"I called Peachie," I told Mom. "And it's okay for me to go."

It was just the time between day and dark.

A big, empty logging truck blasted its horn as it roared by on its way home.

I smoothed my hair the way Dad does and rang Peachie's doorbell.

"It's open. Come on in, William," Peachie called.

She switched off the TV and we sat together on her couch. There are so many horse pictures and framed awards and blue ribbons hanging on her living room wall that you can hardly see the faded flowered wallpaper. There's a picture of her and Woodie with the Sultan in between them. There's a huge oil

painting of the Sultan—just his head. He was looking right at us as we sat, with his long shy face and
soft eyes, a wreath of flowers around his neck.
Peachie had told me once that it was painted from a
photo of him after he won at Del Mar. The Sultan
didn't look stuck on himself at all. Anybody would
love that horse.

I asked about him.

"He's all right. Nervous. If your dog had gotten
into the barn with him today, I'd have a dead horse
out there."

"Peachie," I began. My voice was so gravelly I had
to stop and give a little cough. "Peachie, I'm awfully
sorry about what Riley did. But I want to tell you
honestly, and I'm not just saying this because Riley is
my dog . . . I mean was . . ." I needed another small
cough before I could go on. "I don't think Riley
wanted to hurt the Sultan." I held one of her couch
cushions against my stomach to help me stop shaking. It was a needlepoint pillow, and I glanced down
at it and quickly put it back on the couch beside me.
In red and blue stitches it said, "Who says a dog is a
man's best friend?" There were two needlepointed
horses' heads under the words. Maybe Peachie had
even made it.

Everything I'd planned to say leaped right out of my head.

"Go get yourself a glass of water, William," Peachie said.

I thought maybe I'd just go home, but I couldn't. This was for Riley.

I started again. "The thing is, Peachie, I think Riley wanted to play. You saw the way he looked at the barn door, with his tail wagging and everything. Maybe back sometime when he was a puppy, he had a friend who had a horse. And maybe they ran races together and played tag, stuff like that."

Peachie watched me from the couch and the picture of the Sultan of Kaboor watched me from the wall. I poked my finger in and out of a hole in the knee of my jeans, hoping for some kind of inspiration. Peachie had pushed her rollaway table to the side. There was an empty plate and glass on it and another plate that held Mom's brownies. She reached over and offered the brownie plate to me.

"They're very good," she said.

"I know. Betty Crocker double chocolate chocolate chip," I said. I took a bite, managed to swallow it, and said, "I bet if we got Riley back and really . . . really introduced him to the Sultan and let the

Sultan see what a nice dog he is . . ." I stopped because Peachie was shaking her head.

"I'm sorry, William. A dog that chases livestock is not welcome in this neighborhood. Do you remember what happened to that poor man from Riverton up at Points Pass?"

I remembered, but I just hung my head. A dog had gotten into a pasture and chased a cow. The cow ran right through a barbed-wire fence onto the road, and a man in a Cadillac saw it coming, but too late. He tried to swerve, but hit the cow and then a tree, and by the time the paramedics got to them, the cow and the driver were both dead.

"Riley's not like that," I said. I was desperate. "He's really, really . . ." I fished in my pocket. "Look, Peachie. I want to show you this. I've got all this money in the bank and I want you to have it . . . I'll ride in and take it all out tomorrow. It's for your pain and suffering. And for Doctor Webb's visit. Also, I'm having a birthday in October and I'll have another fifty dollars. . . ."

Peachie touched my cheek with her fingers. "Sweet William," she said. "Remember how I used to call you that when you were little?"

I nodded, gulping back tears.

"William . . . I would never take any money from you. I don't need money. All I need is my house and land here and my old horse to share it with me. If you got your dog back, we'd be living in fear. I can't cope with that and neither can the Sultan. I know you love that dog, but, William, it can't be. I will not change my mind on that."

"They're going to kill him in five days," I said loudly.

"William, to kill an animal isn't done easily by anybody. But it's the law for a good reason."

I stood up, knocking the brownie on the floor and accidentally squashing it into the rug. "You're mean," I said. "I thought you were my friend. It's you who's killing my dog and you don't care. I'll never speak to you ever again. Ever. Never."

I let the door bang hard behind me.

"I'll never speak to you again ever either, Sultan," I shouted toward the barn. "And I'm going to save my dog without anybody's help. I've got five days and I'm going to do it."

## Chapter 9

Dad stayed till I came home. Not that I cared. Not that I cared about anything except Riley.

"How did it go?" he asked.

I headed straight for the stairs. "Bad," I said over my shoulder.

"You don't want to talk about it?" Mom asked.

I was at the bend in the stairs.

"She wants him dead, that's all."

"I have to leave," Dad called. "Do I get a hug good-bye?"

"Bye," I said without turning around. He was the one who'd given Riley to the animal-control people. He was the one who'd told Mom, "William will just have to accept this." Sure. Easy for him. Riley wasn't his dog.

I threw myself on my bed, put on my earphones,

and played the music so loud that it hurt my head. But it didn't drown out my thoughts.

Where was Riley now? Was he in a cage, all alone, wondering where I was, lonely for me the way I was lonely for him? Would we ever see each other again? I buried my face in my pillow that smelled doggy and musky. I'd never let Mom wash this pillowcase. Never.

I heard her banging on the door through the blast of music and I took off the earphones. "Yes?"

"You have an e-mail from Grace," she said. "Why don't you come down and read it?"

"Has Dad gone?"

"Yes. He says he'll stay in touch."

"Great!" I said sarcastically. "That's because he gets in touch with us so often."

There was silence outside the door. "William," she said at last. "You may feel you can blame your father for some things. But this is not one of them."

I rolled my eyes. I'd blame anybody I liked. I'd blame the whole darn world.

Our computer sits on its little table in one corner of the kitchen. There were two e-mail messages in the mailbox, one for Mom about the teachers' get-together that they have in Laird's Restaurant every summer and the one to me from Grace.

"William," it said. "I heard what happened to
Riley and I'm really truly sorry. Mea Culpa, Mea
Culpa, Mea Culpa. I'll be over in the morning." She
signed it "Grace" with a "(Dis)" in parentheses in
front of it. Disgrace. Well, she ought to feel disgraced
after saying all those dumb things about my dog.

Three Mea Culpas are powerful stuff. One is of
medium importance, two is stronger, and three is the
ultimate and highest possible apology. Three means
you are sorry to the ends of the earth, and because it's
so powerful, the other person is committed to forgive
instantly. "I forgive," I muttered, and I sat down and
sent her an e-mail that said, "OK. Come early."

Mom sat at the table, drinking a cup of tea;
the pot with its tea cozy was beside her. It had to be
pretty strong tea by now unless she'd made fresh.

She patted the chair next to her. "Stay for a
minute, William, and let's talk. Can you tell me what
Peachie said?"

I told her in detail because I remembered every
single horrible word. "And I'll never speak to her
again in my entire life," I added.

"Of course you will," Mom said. "Peachie is only
protecting the horse she loves. You know he is almost

the only link to Woodie that she has left. And that makes him doubly precious. Think about all the good things she's done for us."

I didn't want to think, so I began whistling.

Mom kept talking anyway. "Remember when we both had the flu at the very same time and Peachie came every day and brought us soup, and read to you, and even shampooed my hair for me? Peachie is our good, true friend. We have to try to understand."

I stopped whistling, but I didn't say anything.

Mom sipped the last of the tea in her cup and turned the cup upside down on the saucer. She loves to read her tea leaves, which is why we always buy loose tea and not bags. She says reading tea leaves is baloney and we shouldn't believe it; she certainly does not. But it's fun. I think secretly she does believe it a little, and I do too.

She left the cup turned upside down and took my hand. I don't mind her taking my hand as long as it is in private.

"First thing in the morning, I'm going to call that nice man at the pound where we got Riley. Do you remember him? His name is Stephen."

"Yeah? How do you know his name?"

"He told me," Mom said. "We've talked a couple

of times. So I'll call him and ask him if he has any suggestions about what we should do."

"Good. Grace said he liked you."

"Well, I hope he did, because I'm counting on him to give us some good advice."

I felt a quiver of hope. "I bet he will know what to do. And Riley's right there, in his pound. We can ask Stephen if he's okay. And maybe, since he likes you, he'll go in and pet Riley and talk to him so he won't be so lonely. And he could tell him we didn't want him to have to go back and . . ." Tears were puddling behind my eyes. I pulled my hand from Mom's and took an apple from the bowl on the table so I'd have it to chew on and the stupid tears would stop.

"To appeal, I think we'll need a lawyer," Mom said. "I'll ask Stephen."

"Yeah, a lawyer. Let's get the best. I have money."

"William." Mom's voice was very serious. "I have to get something straight with you. I'll do anything I can to spare Riley's life. I was fond of him, too, you know that."

I chewed and chewed on my bite of apple. Something not good was coming! I could feel it in the air.

"But this appeal has to be only to save his life.

Nothing else. We can't have him back here under any circumstances. Whatever you feel now about Peachie, she's right. She would be living in her own home in fear that the dog would get to the Sultan again. That's not fair. We can't do that to her. But if we could stop them from putting Riley to sleep, and then maybe Stephen could find a good home for him someplace else, would that be enough?"

"No!" I shouted.

But then I began imagining.

Sometimes I think my imagination is too extreme. In my mind I saw Riley stretched out on a cold stone table, stiff and dead. I got up and put the rest of the apple into the wastebasket. I'd settle for anything but that.

"If we can just save his life," I said, "I won't try to get him back."

"Good." Mom smiled a shaky smile. "So tomorrow we'll get started. We've only got five days, William."

"I know," I said. "I heard."

"You did?"

"I was coming down the stairs."

Mom was quiet, probably wondering what else I'd heard. All the time we'd been talking, she'd been turning her teacup round and round.

"Are you going to read the leaves?" I asked.

"Sure."

I went over to stand behind her. She held the cup at arm's length, looking into it.

At first, when you look, you see only a mess of black leaves, small as dead ants. But if you squinch your eyes and let go of your thoughts, you begin to see leaf pictures—a flower, a sailboat, or a tree. Right after Grandpa died, I saw a star. It made me feel better, as if Grandpa was telling me he was up there and okay. Once there was a perfect tea-leaf heart, and I thought that maybe meant Mom and Dad were going to get back together. But of course it didn't mean that at all.

"See anything?" I asked. Now we were both peering into the cup.

"Look," I said. "Isn't that a bird? There, close to the handle."

"It could be," Mom said hesitantly.

"It is a bird, flying free." I pointed, tracing in space the way its wings were spread, the way its head was lifted. "It's a sign, Mom. Freedom, right? It would have been better if there'd been a dog running, but the leaves are tricky, right? A dog running would be too obvious."

Mom looked up at me. "Honey, you know we see what we want to see. It's, well, it's kind of wishful thinking." Then she smiled. "It could have been a bird." She put the cup down and I hugged her as she sat, my face buried in her hair in back. She always smells of the sandalwood soap she buys in Lowes' Drugstore. It's her smell.

"It's going to be all right," I whispered.

I felt much better. Riley had me on his side and Mom and Grace and maybe the pound man, Stephen. Now he'd have a lawyer, the best that money could buy.

And then there was the bird. I wouldn't let myself think that was wishful thinking. It was a sign and I believed it.

# Chapter 10

It rained all night. I listened to it patter on the back porch roof, the roof Riley had jumped from. Our fishpond would be a swamp of muddy water again, ugly and dirty. I lay there thinking how hard it was to let go of the pond and I understood that was because it was my last link to Grandpa, in the way the Sultan was Peachie's last link to her dead husband. When things had been good with Riley, I'd thought I could start to let go. I had Riley to fill the empty space. But I didn't have him any longer. I buried my face in my pillow.

Mr. Mysterious, the owl who lives in our old oak tree, called mournfully in the dark. Grace says he isn't an owl, he's a dove and she knows that for sure. We've never seen him, but I know he's an owl, sitting high and dry in his tree, his big yellow eyes watching the rain.

I couldn't sleep, and after a while I got up, found my school notebook that I hadn't opened since school let out, and began making notes. There were lots of things we could do to help the lawyer we were going to get. I made a list and it looked good. "Yeah!" I said.

When I couldn't think of another thing to add to it, I got back in bed. I felt pretty optimistic and fell asleep right away.

Grace came over after eight the next morning. I was eating waffles and honey. Mom popped two more into the toaster for Grace.

"I know I said mean things about Riley," Grace said. "But I didn't think they'd take him back to the pound. I didn't think they'd kill him. I'm overcome with sorrow." Grace talks especially fancy when she's embarrassed, and she was embarrassed now.

"You triple Mea Culpa-ed," I said. "Let's forget about it."

"Well, I want you to know I'm still sorry for the Sultan of Kaboor," Grace said. "And I'm still his friend and Peachie's, too." She picked up three apples out of the bowl on the table and began juggling them, hopping around the kitchen. I have to say she's a pretty good juggler. "I stopped in to see them. . . . *Oops*." She'd dropped one of the apples and interrupted herself to pick it up.

"We have to eat those, you know," I reminded her.

"I stopped in to see them on the way here."

I shrugged. "I don't care. You can like them if you want. I don't have to."

I took the spoon out of the honey jar and licked it, and Mom said, "William!" and Grace said, "How gross! Don't put it back in. I don't want your cooties." Things were back to normal. Sort of.

"So what are we going to do?" Grace asked.

"Well, Mom's going to call Stephen . . ."

"Right," Mom said. "It's eight thirty. I think I should call now." She went to the phone.

"Who's Stephen?" Grace whispered.

"The pound man," I whispered back, and Grace batted her eyelashes. "I told you," she mouthed.

We listened as Mom reached Stephen and explained what had happened with Riley. "Oh, you found out already," she said. Then there was just a bunch of yeses and "I understand's." "I'd really appreciate that," she said at last.

Grace and I crowded around her to see what she was writing down. "Joel Bell," she wrote. Under it she printed a phone number. "Thank you so much, Stephen. You've really helped."

He was talking again and she was listening. She gave a little giggle. Grace and I stared at each other. Mom does not usually make that kind of silly sound.

"No, I don't think that at all," she said. "And I would like to see you again. But right now isn't a good time. After all this is settled . . ." She paused and then said, "I definitely will tell him. You've been really nice, Stephen."

Grace put her hand over her heart and rolled her eyes and made kissing sounds. Fortunately, all of that was behind Mom's back. When she hung up the phone, we were sitting all serious at the table.

"What did he say, Mom?" I asked. I noticed how pink her cheeks were. I wasn't sure how I felt about the way she looked and the way she'd giggled. If Mom got interested in somebody else, then there'd never be a chance of her and Dad getting together again—of us being a family. Of course, this one phone call didn't mean they were going to start dating. And then, I wasn't feeling too great about Dad anyway. And there was old Phoebe.

"Did he ask you out, Mrs. Halston?" Grace asked, all wide eyed and innocent.

"Oh, well . . ." Mom said vaguely, but she pinked even more.

I helped her out. "What was that name you wrote down?"

She put the paper down on the table. "Joel Bell. He's a lawyer. Stephen says he's good and he doesn't charge killer rates. Plus, he put in an appeal for another dog, kind of like Riley's case, a couple years ago, so he has some experience." She went on telling us things—things Stephen thought. Stephen, Stephen. What was this with saying his name so much?

"What about the other dog a couple of years ago? Did he get him off?" I asked.

"Unfortunately, no." Mom sat down. "But that was different. The dog had bitten two people and there was some evidence that it had killed sheep."

I tapped my fingers on the table. "Are we sure that lawyer's all that great? It doesn't sound like it."

"And here's the very best part." She touched the paper with her finger. "Stephen says when there's an appeal, they usually give the dog more time because what if the appeal worked, but it was too late for the dog?"

"How awful!" Grace shuddered.

I couldn't bear to think about it. I couldn't.

"What was it you were supposed to tell me?" I asked. "Something else that Stephen said."

"Oh, yes. He saw Riley this morning, and he's fine and doesn't look too unhappy."

"That's because he doesn't know," I said. "I bet nobody's told him he only has four dog days left to live." I felt like I was choking.

"Well, I wouldn't want to know," Grace said. She counted off on her fingers. "Four days from now is next Saturday. We've got to get started, William."

"I'm going to call Mr. Bell right away," Mom said.

We listened again while she talked to the lawyer.

"Absolutely," she said, and waved for the paper and pencil. "Give me your e-mail address again, please. I'll send the details right away. Thank you so much for taking us on."

When she hung up she told us, "Mr. Bell has a son and a dog too. He says he knows how we feel. He's going to get that appeal in as quickly as possible. It goes to the county commissioners."

"Who the heck are they?" Grace asked.

Mom shrugged. "Officials. They kind of run the county. They'll be the ones making the decision."

That scared me just to think of it. A bunch of people who didn't know us and didn't know Riley having all that power.

Grace and I helped compose the e-mail letter.

"Tell the lawyer how unreasonable Peachie was," I urged.

But Mom shook her head. "That's not necessary, William. He just needs to have the facts."

When she'd sent it, Grace and I went up to my room and I showed her my list.

I read it out loud:

"'Number one. Write to the judge.'" I considered this. "Strike that. 'Write to the county commissioners. Dear Sirs, et cetera, et cetera.'"

I continued. "'Number two. Grace and I both send e-mails to everybody we know and ask them to send e-mails to their friends about Riley and how he needs to have a full pardon.' And tell them to write to the commissioners. You know, put on the pressure."

Grace grinned. "Wow! Our own World Wide Web covering Planet Earth."

"'Number three. Grace and I make big signs and stand by the bank or by Jane's Market. . . .' Somewhere busy, and we'll have a clipboard and a petition and

we'll get people to sign it. And then we can send all
the names to those commissioner guys, too."

"Perfect," Grace said.

"And then . . ." I stopped. "This is a really great
one. When Riley first came, Mom took some pictures of him and some of him and me. In the yard.
The film's still in her camera. Wouldn't it be neat if
I could rent a billboard? There's one just where
Third Street and Oak meet. There's been nothing
on it for ages. What if I could rent it, and get a big
picture of Riley, and put it up there where everybody
who drives along Third or Oak could see it? And
underneath we'd print DOES THIS DOG DESERVE TO
DIE? And tell them to write and say he should be let
off."

Grace doesn't usually give me admiring looks, so
I was pretty stoked to get this one. "You're resource-
ful," she said. "How did you think of that?"

"I don't know." But I did know. I just didn't want
to say. I'd sat on Peachie's couch and the big beautiful picture of the Sultan of Kaboor had smiled down
on me. I'd thought anybody would love that horse.
Nobody would want to see it hurt. In the nighttime
I'd remembered my Riley's big soft eyes and floppy
ears, and I'd thought anybody would love that dog. If

they could see him, nobody would want him hurt. That's how I got the idea.

"We could do leaflets and stand in Monk's Hill and give them out. We'd have Riley's picture on those, too," I added.

"Let's get on *Oprah*." Grace's face glowed. "Or *Rosie O'Donnell*. Rosie loves sob stories. And I think she likes dogs."

"Yeah!"

We gave each other a high ten, which we figure is twice as meaningful as a high five, and decided to go right away into town. We'd take Mom's film to the photo shop and check out prices.

It was still raining a bit, but if you let the rain stop you in Oregon, you'll never do anything. I felt pretty good. All this planning and figuring! It reminded me of when Grace ran for fifth-grade president; I was her manager and I'd thought up all this cool campaign stuff.

But when I rummaged in my closet for my rain slicker, I found Riley's chewed-up tennis ball in the corner. He must have nosed it in here. I picked it up—it had Riley's tooth marks on it and it was still damp from all his sucking at it. He'd even sleep sometimes with this ball in his mouth. My chest started to ache as if someone had stuck a knife in it.

"Are you coming?" Grace asked impatiently.

"Yeah." I set the ball on the closet shelf.

What if none of this worked? What if, no matter what we did, Riley was gone forever? After all, I'd run a great campaign for Grace. And she still lost.

*Chapter 11*

The appeal went in. Riley was given twenty-one days while those commissioners debated his fate. I wasn't allowed to see him. That was part of the decision. It was a hard part, but still.

Mom and Grace and I were ecstatic. Even my dad seemed pleased when he called. Peachie had spoken to Mom. Mom said Peachie told her how sorry she was that I was upset. "But my horse is my only concern," she'd said. "And that's an end to it."

"Well, it's not an end to it," I'd said to Mom, and I'd held my magazine in front of my face to show it didn't matter to me what Peachie thought.

"And now," I told Grace, "we have twenty-one days and a bunch of things to do."

"Too bad about the billboard," Grace said.

"Yeah, well, it figures. Who'd believe an insurance company would book it just when we wanted it?"

"Inevitable," Grace agreed.

It was still raining, because once it starts in this part of the world, it takes its time stopping.

We didn't care. We put on our slickers and cycled through puddles as big as lakes, trying to stay clear of the trucks and cars that sizzled past us, splashing us with muddy water.

We were in a good mood because now we had time, and we were beginning to feel that since we'd won the first battle, we'd for sure win the war. Especially with all our awesome ideas.

The pictures of Riley turned out to be stupendous, so perfect they made both of us choke up. It's nice with Grace. I don't have to worry about showing her my feelings, and it's the same for her with me.

"It's okay," I told her. "Cry if you want."

"It's okay," she told me. "Cry if *you* want."

I asked Mr. Bingham, who owns the photo shop, how much it would cost to blow one up to poster size.

"Thirty-four dollars," he said. "It takes about ten days."

"Ten days! That's cutting it awful close." Grace subtracted out loud. "Ten from twenty-one leaves only eleven."

"Can't you hurry it up?" I asked.

"Uh-uh. They have to be sent in to Medford."

"We're working to save a dog's life," I told Mr. Bingham.

I wiped my wet hand on my dry shirt under the slicker and handed him one of the pictures.

He held it away from him and squinted down. "I get it. This is the dog that's in trouble. I heard about him. A couple of women were talking about him in here this morning. People will have mixed feelings about what happened, William. There are two sides to everything, you know? And the side you're on isn't necessarily right."

"But my dog's innocent," I said loudly. "Look at him."

"I am looking." Mr. Bingham stared long distance at Riley's picture.

"Tell you what," he said. "I'll give them a call at the lab and ask them to put a rush on these for you. Want it for your room, do you?"

"Eventually." Grace gave me a warning look. I guessed it was better not to broadcast our plans.

"I was very sorry about your grandpa," Mr. Bingham said to me. "He was a nice man. We were in the same bowling league."

I nodded. "Thursday nights. The Sunshine

Bowlers." And I was remembering Grandpa in his yellow sweatshirt, heading out the door on Thursday nights, whistling. I had that empty feeling in my stomach again.

Mr. Bingham smiled and patted my shoulder. "I'm not going to charge you for the photos you got today. They're on the house. I have a dog myself."

"Gee, thanks," I said.

"You're welcome."

We were just about to leave, still looking at the pictures, when the bell above the door rang and Ellis Porter and Duane Smith came in. Rain blew in with them. They pushed back the hoods of their jackets.

"What you got there?" Ellis asked in that nasty way he has. He and Duane are in high school now, but we know them from last year.

Before I could even speak, Duane snatched the pictures out of my hand.

"Here now, here now," Mr. Bingham said anxiously.

"Aw, he's got pretty dog pictures." Duane held them high above his head. Duane's as tall as a lamppost, so when I say high, I mean high.

Grace clawed at his arm. "Give them back, you dweeb!"

Duane squinted down at her and grinned. "This

your little friend's killer dog?"

Ellis had taken some of the pictures from him, scowling at them and at us. "I hate dogs," he said. "Dogs are vermin."

"They are not." I jumped, trying to get at the pictures, which wasn't easy because Ellis is just about as tall as Duane, only wider.

Mr. Bingham had come around the counter, small and neat in his tweed jacket. He held out his hand. "Let's have the pictures. Right now. I mean it."

Ellis let them slide from his grasp, and as soon as he did, Duane did, too. They fanned out all over the floor.

"*Oops,*" Ellis said, and Duane gave this hideous guffaw.

Riley's face smiled up at me, from the floor, all doggy grin and wet, pink tongue. If anybody stepped on him, I'd . . .

"Did you ever hear about my cat?" Ellis asked, and he wasn't guffawing like Duane or even smiling. He looked like a giant standing there, his legs spread apart, glaring down at us where we groveled on the floor, picking up one picture after another.

"Your cat?" Grace asked.

"Yeah, my cat."

I squinted up at him.

His voice was so cold and deadly it fluttered shivers along my spine.

"My cat's name was Josephine. I had her since first grade."

Ellis stopped, and it was suddenly so quiet I could hear a faucet drip, drip, dripping somewhere in the back of the shop. Or maybe it was a rain gutter outside in the alley.

"Josephine was lying on the roof of my dad's truck, sleeping, when these three dogs came along the street, no leashes, no nothing."

Something awful was coming next. I could feel it slither between us.

"Riley was always on a leash," I whispered.

Duane nodded. "Sure, sure. He was on a leash when he attacked that poor old lady's horse."

"She's not a poor old lady," Grace said. "Don't be so insulting when you don't even know her."

"Oh, so sorry," Duane whimpered.

"My cat was old, all right," Ellis said. "She was sound asleep when those dogs went after her. They pulled her down off the truck. They played with her like she was some kind of stuffed toy. When they left, she was dead."

I was frozen there on the floor. The faucet still

dripped, big fat drops. I wished Mr. Bingham would go make it stop. Of course, if it was the gutter running, he couldn't make it stop.

I managed to stand. My shoes squelched water. I hadn't noticed how wet they were, and the bottom of my jeans, too.

"That was awful about your cat," I said. "But you can't judge all dogs by—"

"I can judge yours," Ellis said. "He would have likely torn that horse apart except it was too big for him."

"That horse probably kicked him good," Duane added.

"Please leave." Mr. Bingham looked puny next to Ellis.

"For all I know, that killer of yours could have been one of the three that got Josephine," Ellis said.

I glared at him. "He wasn't."

"Riley has a sweet disposition and temperament," Grace said, and Duane gave that awful guffaw again.

"Temperament and disposition? You swallow a dictionary or something?"

I hated that guffaw. It sounded like a sick donkey braying.

Mr. Bingham had gone around the counter and

picked up his phone. "Leave right now or I'm calling the police."

"We're going, we're going," Duane said. "Hold on to your hair."

Ellis was watching me closely. "How long have you had that dog?" He touched the white scar above his lip, the one Grace says gives him that "evil Ellis look."

"I've had him long enough," I said.

"Yeah? Was he a stray?"

"No, but . . ." I stopped.

He was thinking ahead of me. "You got him in the pound, I bet. Over in Portland. Why do you think somebody took him there in the first place? Not because he was an angel, that's for sure."

"They were moving," I began.

"Sure, sure."

Mr. Bingham gestured with the phone. "I'm going to count to ten," he said. "One. Two . . ."

The bell above the door rang, and Mrs. Upton, who goes to our church, came in. Mrs. Upton's really nice. She brings candy every year on the Sunday before Halloween and hands it out to the kids. Good stuff, too. Mars Bars. Milky Ways.

"Hello, William," she said, chirpy as a bird. "Enjoying your vacation?" She put her big umbrella behind the door and took a scarf off her hair. "A great day for ducks."

"C'mon." Ellis humped his big shoulders, and he and Duane moved toward the door. "I'm glad the old lady's getting your dog killed," he said back at me. "The sooner the better."

Mrs. Upton was making little horrified clucking noises.

"You're a jerk and you know it," I said too loudly. I wasn't feeling sorry for him anymore. I stuck out my lower lip, which I do when I'm really mad, and which Grace says makes me look fierce. "It's not going to happen."

"Oh, yeah?" That was Duane. "Who's going to stop the execution? The pope?"

"We're going to stop it." I put the pictures I'd picked up behind my back as if I could shield them, as if they were Riley.

"And you know who's going to stop you stopping it?" Ellis imitated my voice, sticking out his lip the way I'd done. He answered his own question. "We are. And there'll be plenty of people ready to help us."

"You boys have really bad attitudes." Mrs. Upton squinted at Ellis. "Are you Beth Porter's son? She'd be ashamed of you."

Ellis gave her one of his hateful looks. "Let's go," he said again to Duane.

They pulled up the hoods of their jackets and were gone.

Mrs. Upton looked dazed. "What was all that about?"

Grace had dashed to the door and jerked it open so furiously that the bell went crazy, jangling its head off. She stepped outside. The rain was coming down like a cloudburst, but Grace didn't seem to notice.

"You two guys think you're so *that*," she yelled. "You're not. We despise you. And we're going to save Riley. You'll see."

She came back in, shaking water off herself the way Riley used to when he got wet.

"Oh, my!" Mrs. Upton said to me. "Was that your dog that chased the horse? I didn't realize." She paused. "Well, it is a problem, isn't it? I certainly can understand why Mrs. Peachtree . . ."

"Peachwood," I said.

"Yes. Well, we can't really allow dogs to chase livestock around here. There are too many . . ." She stopped. "You don't need to hear all this again, I'm sure."

She smiled, but she'd said enough so I knew which side she was on. And Mrs. Upton was nice, the Halloween candy and all.

I had this sudden awful understanding that there'd be others, nice and not so nice, who felt the same way. What was it Mr. Bingham had said? "There are two sides to everything. And the one you're on isn't necessarily right."

# Chapter 12

T wenty-one days and no time to waste.

We had plans.

The first morning, Grace did a flyer on my computer. She's better at stuff like that than I am. It read:

THIS DOG WAS UNJUSTLY CONDEMNED
TO DIE. CALL 555-6432 AND DEMAND
THAT HIS LIFE BE SPARED.

I thought that sounded a bit bossy, but Grace said it had the ring of authority, and that's what we needed. We left a space at the top for Riley's picture and cycled to the copy shop to have two hundred made on bright, eye-popping yellow paper.

Our first shock came when the copy guy asked, "What is all this? Animal Rights Day or something?

I did another one of these this morning, with a horse on it."

Grace gasped. "Oh, no. Ellis Porter and Duane Smith are making flyers, too. Those dweebs."

"What did that one say?" I asked.

The copy guy shrugged. "I never looked. I remember the horse, though. Old-looking nag."

"That nag's a thoroughbred," I said, grabbing our flyers. "Come on, Grace. We've got to move fast."

We walked along Main Street in the rain, asking every store owner if he'd put one of our flyers in his window. And that's when we got our second shock. Only one would, and that was Seedy's CD Emporium. I guess he said yes because I'm such a good customer.

"But how come *you* won't?" Grace asked Mr. Bingham in the photo shop. "I mean, you were so nice about Riley's pictures."

Mr. Bingham spread his hands. "It's not that easy, young lady. I'm a businessman and I don't take sides. Not in public, anyway. No politics, no religion, nothing controversial."

"At least none of the dweebs' flyers are up either," Grace said, and that comforted us.

"Let's go home, eat lunch, and get to our next strategy," I said.

Mom opened two cans of chili for us and melted so much cheese on top that it dripped down the sides of the bowl. Then she toasted bread for us to dip in it. My mom is truly the best cook the world has ever seen.

"Your mother called," she told Grace. "You're not to forget you have your flute lesson at four thirty. And William, your dad called too."

"What for?" I asked. "To see if Riley's dead yet?"

Grace glared. "You don't have to be so mean."

"He just wanted to know how you were holding up," Mom said quietly.

I didn't answer.

Grace and I worked all afternoon sending e-mails to everyone we knew who had an e-mail address. We copied word for word the message on our flyer. Then we folded fifty of the bright yellow sheets and addressed them to friends and neighbors and anyone else whose listing we found in Mom's phone book. Not Peachie, though. I sat, looking at her name and number, feeling this miserable mixture of sadness and anger. Horrible old Peachie, I thought. This is your fault! But somehow my thoughts didn't sound all that sincere, even to myself. Maybe because things didn't seem so hopeless anymore.

"I wonder what Ellis and Duane are doing now," Grace asked, licking stamps and putting them on our folded flyers. She used her closed fist to thump each stamp in place. "Bam! Take this, Ellis! Bam! Take this, Duane," she muttered, and that made Mom and me laugh.

There were three great piles of folded flyers on the table, and Mom touched one of them with the tip of her finger, careful not to knock it over. "Talk about covering the waterfront," she said cheerfully.

"Talk about no stone unturned," Grace added.

"Talk about no bridge left uncrossed," I added, though I wasn't sure that made much sense.

Grace took the flyers to mail when she left. "I'll kiss each one for luck before I drop it through the slot," she said, and I went, "*Yuck*, poison in your mailbox."

When she'd gone, I made a calendar and taped it on the side of the refrigerator below the lawyer's card. We weren't hearing much from him, but Mom said that was all right. It was the way lawyers worked. He'd be biding his time, but we could be sure he was preparing his case. I hoped he was working his buns off.

There were twenty-one squares on the calendar, one for every day Riley had left. I X-ed out the first one in red. One day used up, twenty to go. And I tried hard not to look at the last square, not to think what it meant. All day long I'd tried not to see Riley's face on our flyers. I'd tried to make this a sort of game, a challenge, and not remember what the reward would be or what would happen if we lost.

When Grandpa and I were starting on the pond, he'd say to me, "We can't do it all in one day, Willie Boy. One step at a time. Just keep going." I'd remember. One step at a time. And I'd keep going.

Stephen, the pound man, called Mom that night. She looked happy and young when she talked to him, and that was another strange thing worth thinking about. If it hadn't been for Riley, they'd never have met. It was too early yet to figure out if that was a plus or a minus.

"How is Riley?" I heard her ask him, and then she held the phone away and said to me, "Riley's fine. Stephen says he's eating well and he doesn't seem to be moping."

"Ask him . . . ask him . . ." I began. But I didn't know what else I *could* ask him. "Does Riley miss me? Does he miss our runs in the woods? Does he remember the day at the river when he saved me? Does he miss sleeping with me, his head on the pillow next to mine?" But how could the pound man know the answers? And then I had a brainstorm and I leaped out of my chair.

"Mom! Mom! I know I'm not supposed to see Riley . . . like I've got head lice or something. But couldn't Stephen smuggle me in? I could wear a disguise, even. I mean, Stephen's your friend and he works there. Who would recognize me anyway? If I could just see Riley again, stroke him, let him lick my face." I stopped. In a minute I was going to bawl. I tried to grab the phone. "Let me talk. . . ."

"Honey! Honey!" Mom fended me off, and her face was so loving and understanding that I knew I definitely *was* going to bawl.

On the phone I could hear Stephen saying my name, and Mom handed the phone over to me.

I swallowed hard.

Stephen's voice, so close he could have been in the kitchen with us, said, "William? I know you want to see your dog. But believe me, it would be the wrong thing to do. You agreed to that. Riley's on . . . well, he's kind of on parole now. You don't want to break the rules and spoil it for him. It's not worth the chance."

Mom stood close and very still, her lips pressed tightly as if she might cry herself.

"It's not fair," I muttered.

"You know something," Stephen said, "it *is* fair. They've given you extra time, a chance to get the commissioners to change their minds. They've leaned over backward for you." He paused. "Right?"

I wasn't going to say right. Not one bit of this was right.

I gave the phone back to Mom, went to the refrigerator, and poured myself a glass of milk. I looked hard at those big squares. The life calendar. One down. Lots of time left.

Did Ellis Porter have a calendar too, and was he staring at it, planning as I was planning?

A life for a life.

A dog for his cat.

It didn't matter to him which dog. Riley would do fine.

*Chapter 13*

T
he next morning we taped a flyer on every lamppost and tree along Main Street. The rain had stopped, the sun was out, and the big yellow notices were eye-popping all right. "Better even than having them in windows," Grace said admiringly. "No glass to get in the way."

We stood on opposite sidewalks, giving out flyers to anyone who passed by who would take one. Some did. Some didn't. Some said, "Good luck!" or "I was sorry about your dog." But others didn't look at us, staring straight ahead as if we were invisible. Others muttered stuff like, "A dog that chases another animal gets no sympathy from me," or worst of all, "Give it up, kid. You're wasting your time. The dog's a goner."

"No," I said. "No."

Some looked so angry it made my heart beat fast,

and sometimes they'd take a flyer and crumple it up and toss it into the gutter. When they did, I'd pick it up, and if it wasn't too creased, I'd use it again. If it was, I'd stick it in my backpack to take home. What if I was the one accused of littering?

But there were nice passersby, too. A woman who'd been at the ATM gave me a twenty-dollar bill. "Here, son," she said. "This will help with expenses."

"Thanks," I told her, and I could have thrown my arms around her and hugged her, except that might have embarrassed her to death. She was wearing a big hat and actually she reminded me of Peachie.

A little kid held up his puppy to me. "His name is Spot. You can pet him if you like," he said.

I kissed the top of the puppy's head and it had a Riley dog smell.

And then I heard Grace shout, "Yo, William!" from the other side of the street, and I looked where she was pointing. There were Ellis Porter and Duane Smith, farther up Main, giving out flyers that definitely weren't ours. Theirs was an ugly shade of pink, but eye-popping too. I knew the picture of the Sultan was on theirs. And what else?

I didn't have to wait long to find out. Jim Deppe, who's in my grade, came zipping along on his bike

and handed me one. "Take a gander," he said, and
rode off.

There, on that sick-making pink paper, was a picture of the Sultan of Kaboor, old and weary-looking,
standing by Peachie's fence. His head drooped. There
was a bandage on one leg. Underneath the picture,
the flyer said:

THIS HORSE WAS CHASED ALMOST TO DEATH
BY A VICIOUS, UNLEASHED DOG, NAME OF RILEY.
UPHOLD THE DEATH PENALTY FOR ALL DOGS
THAT CHASE OUR LIVESTOCK. CALL 555-6432
AND DEMAND THAT THE LAW IS OBEYED.
SIGN OUR PETITION.

Chased almost to death! What a lie! Several people were coming along the sidewalk, reading as they
walked. "That isn't even true," I told them desper-
ately. "My dog isn't vicious. He's . . . look . . . here's a
picture of him . . . does he . . ."

"Did he chase this horse or not?" a red-faced man
with a red mustache asked me.

I scrunched my shoulders. "He did. But he didn't
hurt . . ."

"'Nuff said." He swung on his heel.

∞     ∞     ∞

That night Grace and I decided we should get our
petition ready fast. Tomorrow we'd have people sign
ours. How many would be willing to sign to have
Riley saved? I wasn't so sure anymore. Would Ellis and
Duane be back tomorrow or would one day of standing out there on Main Street be enough for them?

They were there when we got to Main Street the
next day at ten after nine. But our yellow flyers had
all disappeared from the trees and telephone poles.

Grace and I marched up to Duane and Ellis. "You
took down our notices, didn't you?" I said.

"Us?" Duane gave a little titter. "We wouldn't do
a thing like that."

"You know we're just going to put them up again,"
Grace said.

"You know we're just going to take them down
again," Ellis mocked. It was amazing the way he
could make himself sound like Grace, only soppy and
silly.

I stuck out my lip. "It's illegal to take those
down," I said. "You'll see. I'm going to talk to our
lawyer."

Ellis hooted with laughter, and Duane joined in.
"Your lawyer? Give me a break."

"Come on, Grace," I said.

And then I noticed something I hadn't really noticed before. There were more people on Main Street than usual for this early in the morning. They gathered in small clusters along the sidewalk, talking loudly, even angrily. I heard bits of conversations. "If this dog gets off . . . what happens next time?" ". . . my two lambs last spring up on Plain Meadow?" "Wasn't that coyotes?" "Coulda been. Coulda been a dog, though." "Yeah, well, I have two collies that would never . . ."

Grace and I pushed our way between them. They stopped talking till we had passed.

"What's happening?" Grace whispered to me.

"I think they're taking sides," I whispered back.

"Yeah. But I don't see too many on ours," Grace muttered.

We stood where we'd stood yesterday. A man moved close to me. He had a handmade banner that said THOU SHALT NOT KILL.

For a minute I didn't know whether he was talking about Riley, or all those dead lambs, but then he said, "Is it okay if I stand behind you with this?" I realized he was for us, and I nodded. "Sure, help yourself."

Main Street was lined with cars. Kids from school stopped by to talk to us. "Man! That Ellis Porter! He's such a toad! Gimme your petition and I'll sign it."

I had a feeling the signers had to be registered voters or at least over eighteen, but I was happy to take every name I could get.

A man stopped and asked me if I knew about red pepper. "Put it on your dog's nose every time he looks at another animal and he'll not go near it," he said.

"Really?"

He nodded. "Try it when you get him back."

I held on to those words, saying them over and over to myself. "When I get him back."

We cycled home for peanut butter toast and cherries and a rest on the porch. Riley used to lie there on the step, snapping at flies. Sometimes he'd rest his head on the big roll of butyl liner. Where was he lying now?

"I'm tired," Grace said.

"Me too."

We sat in the cool for a while, drinking iced tea. It comes from a package, but Mom puts lemon slices and mint leaves in it and it's delicious. I could hear her in the kitchen, working on the computer.

Grace pushed lazily in the glider. "Sure would be

nice to take the afternoon off."

"I'm not going to."

After a minute, she said, "I'm not either."

We picked up our bikes and wheeled back down the driveway, past Peachie's house. She was nowhere to be seen, but the Sultan was peacefully grazing over by the barn. Peachie's roses were in bloom against the fence. Would she bring bunches of them to us this year? Mom loves them so much. "They smell like summer," she says.

I felt this awful suffocating sadness, as if everything in the world were wrong and nothing would ever be the same again. "Sweet William," Peachie used to call me, and I had this faraway memory of when I was very small and Peachie would call out to me, "Over here, Sweet William."

I reached inside me for that cold anger I'd felt against her, and I had trouble finding it. She'd done it, though. She'd told on Riley. Never mind the Sweet William thing. I pedaled harder.

There were still lots of people on the sidewalks. I figured some of them had gone home for peanut butter toast and iced tea of their own and come back, though I wasn't sure if they were the same ones who'd been around in the morning. I turned to offer

a yellow flyer to a woman in jeans and a striped
T-shirt who was passing, and suddenly realized it
was Peachie. My heart gave a frightened jump.
What would I say to her?

"Oh . . . er . . ." I pulled my hand back, holding
the bunch of flyers against my chest. "Hello,
Peachie."

"William!"

"How . . . how is the Sultan?" I stammered. "I saw
him when I went past your house. I waved to him." I
tried for a grin. "But he didn't wave back."

I was trying to think what I could say next and
wishing Peachie would just go on into the bank, or
wherever she was planning on going, when a woman
with the spikiest hair I'd ever seen in my life pushed
her face real close to mine. She was so close I could
see the black stuff clumped in her eyelashes.
Tarantula eyes, I thought. In her hand was a microphone.

"William Halston?" she asked with this totally
bogus smile.

"Yes," I said uncertainly.

Behind her was a skinny guy carrying a camera
about as big as he was.

"Awesome," Tarantula Eyes said. "I'm Trixie

Allen, *What's Going On*, seven P.M., Channel Three, Portland. You've probably seen my program?"

I shook my head.

"This is Boots, my cameraman." She pulled the skinny guy forward, jostling Peachie to the side.

"Peachie?" I began.

"Peachie?" Tarantula's tarantula eyes widened. She stole a quick glance down at the notebook she held. "Would that be Mrs. Peachwood, the, shall we say, instigator of this whole affair?"

I was frantically waving Grace over.

"What luck!" Tarantula Eyes smiled a satisfied tarantula smile. She wedged the microphone under her arm and grabbed Peachie's hand. "We planned on calling you. . . . I have a cell phone in my pocket here, never travel without it. . . ." Again that bogus smile. "I hoped to come over to your house right after my interview with William. This is even better, getting the two of you together like this."

Peachie had not said a word and neither had I, but Grace, who'd come over, blurted out, "Is Riley going to be on TV? How cool." Her grin went ear to ear, and she nudged me so hard with her shoulder, I almost fell off the curb.

"Hi, Peachie," she said, and then, realizing that

Peachie wouldn't be thrilled to have Riley on TV, she muttered, "Peachie, this is Trixie Allen of Channel Three," and waved her flyers as if she were introducing them.

"We've met," Peachie said.

Boots was doing something businesslike with his camera. Trixie slithered her smile at Grace. "Are you William's little girlfriend?"

"No," Grace said. "I'm his partner in trying to save Riley. It's great that you're going to do a story on him."

"Good, fine." Trixie consulted her notebook. "Well, now, William and Mrs. Peachwood . . . I'm just going to ask you both a few questions. Can you fill me in? Mrs. Peachwood, as I understand it, your horse . . ."

"I'm sorry, Miss Allen." Peachie's voice was low and absolutely polite. "I don't intend to answer any questions or be interviewed either."

"But I bet you're mad at each other, you and William?" The tarantula smile was back. "Won't you at least . . ."

"I'm not at all mad at William," Peachie said. "William is my good friend. He's looking out for his dog is all. Now, if you'll excuse me . . ."

A little crowd had gathered, spilling onto the street. We watched as Peachie edged through the people and through the doors into the bank.

Miss Allen shrugged. "No problem. William? Why don't *you* just fill our viewers in on the story?"

Boots held up his hand, and Trixie said, "Just a second . . . we're having a little problem here with the picture."

The crowd around us was getting bigger. Grace took my pile of flyers so I'd have my hands free, I wasn't sure for what. I tucked my T-shirt tighter into my jeans.

"She's not Rosie or Oprah," Grace whispered. "But this is fabulous. Too bad we don't have the big photograph of Riley yet."

The man with the Thou Shalt Not Kill banner had moved so he was right behind me. He crouched to make sure he'd be in the picture.

"Ready, William?" Trixie asked.

I nodded.

"Do good," Grace whispered.

"Well," I began, "Riley was the most perfect dog . . . I mean, *is* the most perfect dog. It was just . . ."

I went on and on explaining, not being mean

about Peachie, trying to be fair, just saying how much we all loved the Sultan. Trixie kept nodding and smiling, and now and then butting in with a question. Grace kept giving me thumbs up, and I was just going into how everybody could help save Riley and how if he lived, I'd never have him back here. Not ever, he'd be far away, in the middle of a city maybe, and never chase anything again . . .

"Except maybe his tail," Trixie Allen said humorously, and I nodded.

"He liked to chase his tail. He was funny because he'd catch it and fall over himself." I stopped. How awful if I cried on TV.

And then I turned a little, and for the first time I saw Ellis Porter and Duane Smith on the edge of the crowd. Oh, no. Faster than fast, I moved to block them from Trixie, in case she knew who they were, and then I talked even faster to keep her attention on me.

But, unfortunately, Trixie knew her stuff and had read up on everything before coming here. Her program wasn't called *What's Going On* for nothing.

After I wound down, not able to think of a single other thing to say, she thanked me graciously, then said, "And now we will hear from Mr. Ellis Porter and

Mr. Duane Smith, who have taken up arms on behalf of the old racehorse, the Sultan of Kaboor. I had hoped to bring the Sultan's owner to you this evening, too, but apparently she is too upset over what happened to make a television appearance. Here, again, to speak for her, and for her horse, are Ellis Porter and Duane Smith."

And the awful thing was, there was a little scattering of applause as the crowd made way for them.

Grace said afterward the applause was for me, for how good I'd been presenting Riley's case.

But I didn't think so.

Chapter 14

There's a saying, "Be careful what you wish for . . . you might get it." That must be among the truest sayings in the whole world. Grace and I had wished we could get our story of Riley on TV. And that had happened. But . . . Ellis and Duane had had a chance to tell the other side of the story, too.

That night, Mom and Grace and Grace's mom and dad and her two little brothers, Sam and Colin, and I watched Trixie Allen's program. Ordinarily, if I'd been on TV, Peachie would have been on the couch beside me. Not that ordinarily I would have been on TV. But Peachie used to come over for anything important, like a space shuttle shot, or the night the magician told all the secrets of how the tricks were done. Peachie and Mom and I didn't like him. "He's a spoiler," Peachie said. I tried to sort out the muddle of my Peachie feelings. Of course I was still mad. But I couldn't help remembering good things.

If this had been three months ago, my grandpa would have been here next to me, too. Three years ago, my dad would have been here. Two weeks ago, Riley would have been lying next to me, one paw in my lap, though he and I would have been watching an old *Leave It to Beaver*, not watching about him maybe having to die.

Everything was disappearing from me. It was scary. I felt emptied out.

"Here, William, have a lemon square." Grace passed me the plate. "You were far better than Ellis. You'll see."

That's the best thing about a best friend. She knows when you need cheering up.

We watched. First there was a story about a new bookstore opening in Portland, and Trixie interviewing a Portland woman who's written a children's book, I guess.

And then Grace's mom said, "Everybody shush. Here it is." And I was on.

It's weird listening to yourself. It's weird seeing yourself. I thought I looked real shifty-eyed.

Everybody made comments. Everybody was delighted with me. I couldn't believe how interested Trixie was in my every word, especially when I knew for a fact that once she'd examined her eyelashes in an itty-bitty mirror when the camera was on me, not on her. That photographer must have woven in some good fake-attention shots. It just goes to show you, I thought.

And then we listened to Ellis, who sounded a lot nicer and kinder than he really is. The program cut to a hardware store commercial, and Grace muttered, "At least he didn't talk about his cat."

Sam stopped licking the sticky lemon off his fingers. "What about his cat?"

"Oh." Grace stumbled a bit trying to figure out how much to tell him. "Some mean dogs beat up on his cat, that's all."

Sam's eyes widened. "If some mean dogs did that to our kitty, I'd . . . I'd do something really bad to them."

"Ellis is trying. In a misdirected way," Grace said.

"Why don't you just say the same words other people say, Gracie," Colin complained. "That way we'd understand."

Grace was scowling. "I'm really mad. You said

things to Trixie that she didn't report. She just cut items out. She made your time shorter than theirs. That's not fair. She . . ." Grace stopped talking because Trixie was on again.

"Well, that's all for now," she said. "Be sure to follow this saga of Riley, the condemned dog. Call those commissioners and let them know how you vote. Here's the number again. And hey, call us too. We're going to be taking a poll ourselves because, as you know, we're interested in what's going on in your world today."

"Vote?" I said. My voice quavered. "Polls? This is not a stupid election. This is about my dog."

Grace's dad clapped me on the shoulder. "It's okay. That's just TV talk. You did super well, William."

"Thanks." I truthfully knew I'd done all right in the interview. But nobody was saying what I also knew. Ellis Porter had done all right, too.

"Why didn't you say something, Gracie?" Sam asked.

"Because Miss Trixie wasn't talking to me, dork," Grace snapped.

"I'm proud of you, hon," Mom said. "I'm proud of you for fighting so hard for what you think is right."

Everyone chimed in and it was pretty nice. I didn't feel so emptied out anymore.

I was surprised the next day at how many viewers Trixie had. Mr. Rodriguez from down the road called in the morning, and so did Mrs. Carter, my math teacher, and the box girl in the market, and a bunch of others.

And my dad.

"Well done, son." I imagined him sitting elegantly in his elegant chair in his apartment—which was probably elegant, too.

"Thanks. Somebody has to do something," I said meaningfully. "I mean, apart from pulling Riley down the stairs and shoving him out to the animal-control guys."

"That's not fair, William, and you know it," Dad said. "I hope you succeed."

"Right," I said.

Mom usually acts as if she doesn't hear my kitchen phone conversations, which is pretty hard when we're both in the same room. But this time she didn't pretend. She watched me with a serious face, and as soon as I hung up, she nodded toward the chair at the table, opposite her.

I sat.

"What your dad did with Riley, he did for you. And for me. Riley had to go. Your father didn't want either of us to get into anything with the animal-control people. He knew it would make a bad situation worse. I'm glad he was here. Now let go of the anger you have for him, William. Just let it go."

I drifted a little salt from the shaker onto the table and made a finger design in it, not looking at her.

"It's not just the dog," I began.

"I know it's not just the dog. William . . . people change. Your dad and I parted for good reasons. To tell the truth, we were both miserable. I *tried* to hold on . . ." I sensed her shrug, though I was so busy making my salt into a small pyramid that kept sliding down that I didn't lift my head.

"And for those good reasons, we won't be getting back together. I've faced that."

"Really?" I asked, pausing in the middle of my pyramid-building to give her a quick glance.

"Really. So get rid of that anger. I've gotten rid of mine."

I raised my eyebrows. "You have?"

Mom grinned. "Well, maybe not all of it. And maybe not all of the time."

I grinned back. "Okay. I'll try."

"So next time you see your dad, you might tell him you're sorry for being so hateful on the phone just now."

I scattered the salt. "Oh, sure, next time I see him. And when will that be? He's not exactly on our doorstep." I heard my nasty, sarcastic tone. "Sorry," I muttered.

"Don't tell me sorry. Tell him," Mom said. "And get rid of that salt."

I scooped it into my hand and poured it into the sink.

Before I went to bed that night, I X-ed off another square. Four down, seventeen to go.

The next day I sent our petitions to Mr. Joel Bell to send to the commissioners. Grace and I both figured the commissioners would pay more attention if the signatures came from a lawyer. We had 103 names on those petitions, which seemed pretty good to us, although we wished we knew how many Ellis and Duane had on theirs.

We took the flyers we had left and taped them back on trees and lampposts and walls. But we gave up on giving out any more since person after person just shook their heads.

"I think about everyone has one of them by now," Grace said. I hoped that was the reason and that it wasn't because they were bored with the Riley story. At least not until those twenty-one days were up. Sixteen to go now—and no way to slow them down.

I paid ten dollars to have an ad printed in the *Monk's Hill Gazette* that repeated the phone number to call.

"By now I know that phone number better than my own," Grace's mom said. "Listen to this. I called my husband's office from downtown today and got city hall by mistake."

"Did you speak to . . ." I began.

"Voicemail, of course. But I did leave a good message. Never waste an opportunity, right?"

That night the Channel Three poll votes were announced by a very serious Trixie Allen.

"It's official," she said. "Here's *What's Going On* in your world today." We had to wait while they played a commercial of dancing cows, and then Trixie asked, "And how did you vote? Well, we had a lot of callers on this very divisive question of Riley the dog. Thirty-two of those who responded think Riley's life should be spared. Fifty-four think the execution should proceed as planned."

"How can they?" I whispered. "How can fifty-four people want my dog dead? I told them. He's not going to bother them."

Mom pulled me close. "Shhh, honey. Those votes don't mean a thing. It's not official, whatever she says. The only thing that will matter in the end is what the commissioners decide. And I doubt very much if any of them watch Trixie Allen's show. They're there in the big city, after all."

But I wasn't a bit sure. It seemed to me that a lot of people watched *What's Going On*. Grace and I had thought that would be good. But it wasn't turning out that way. I knew politicians were influenced by polls; even the president watched them. Who was to say county commissioners were any different?

*Chapter 15*

The days and nights were going by.

There were now more Xs on the calendar than there were spaces.

Our flyers were finished, and we debated getting more, but what was the point?

Mr. Bingham from the photo shop called to say the big photograph of Riley had come in.

We got it and taped it onto a humongous piece of cardboard. It was actually from the box that had held the wood for the deck Grandpa and I were planning to build around our pond. I debated about whether or not I should take the wood out and cut up the box, but I thought it would be all right. Grandpa would understand that this was for a good purpose.

For two hours Grace and I marched up and down Main Street, carrying it. Not too many people paid too much attention. We were about to give up and head for home when we saw Ellis and Duane slouching toward us.

"Just walk past," Grace muttered. "Don't even look at them."

Some hope.

They stopped right in front of us, blocking the sidewalk, and because of the cars and trucks parked by the curb, we had no room to step off and go around them.

"Excuse us," I said, jamming my shoulder into Duane's chest.

"Oh, look at the picture they've got now," Ellis said. "Didn't we see this before, Duane? They liked it so much they made it bigger. . . . How cute is that?" His hand shot up and grabbed the bottom of the cardboard, pulling it down, lopsided, between Grace and me.

"You'd better let go," I said.

"Or what?" The picture jerked up and down, one corner of it thumping against the sidewalk.

I dropped my end and shoved Ellis with all my strength.

He sprawled backward and I leaped on top of him.

Cora Putnam came rushing out of the bakery,

carrying a long, skinny bakery loaf in a long, skinny bag.

"Boys! Boys!" she shouted. "What's going on here? Stop it this minute."

She was smacking me hard on the head and I realized she was whacking me with her long, crusty loaf. Crumbs rained down.

I had Ellis pinned underneath me, one knee on his stomach. King of the World, I thought, happier than I'd been in ages.

Above me I heard Grace say, "Get him, William. Sock him good," and then she said, "Quit it, Duane! Let go!" and there was a ripping sound.

I began scrambling up. Cora had dropped her loaf and was pulling on the back of my shirt. A couple of other interested people stood around, gawking.

"Look what you've done, you cockroach!" Grace wailed, and I saw that our big picture of Riley, the one we'd taped so carefully onto the cardboard, had been torn away and was lying in two jagged pieces on the sidewalk.

I stood, looking at the pieces, my heart hammering. All the anger I'd had, all the triumph was gone, and there was nothing inside me but hopelessness. Riley's ripped-up picture seemed like an omen. I clenched my jaws so tightly my face hurt.

Ellis was up now. "Want to do that again?" he asked, his voice filled with fury.

But someone must have taken hold of him from behind. Someone said, "Enough now. There's been enough," and a different voice said, "Why don't you two guys go over and walk on the other side of the street and leave William and Grace be."

I picked up the two torn pieces of the photograph and fitted them together in my hands. Grace had the cardboard, which was bent but not torn.

"Come on," she said to me. "Come on. We can go home and glue it on again. That'll work."

I shook my head. The picture was finished. I wished I didn't have the scary thought that Riley was finished, too.

But I couldn't give up, not as long as there was any chance. There were other things I could do.

I wrote a letter to the editor of the *Courier* and he printed it. I was so jazzed, I wrote two more, but I guess the editor felt there was no need to overdo it. Anyway, he didn't print them. And somebody called Joseph Olson wrote an answer to my first letter that said, "So we just shift our problem off onto some other unsuspecting farmer? Pass Riley along. Let's see how many horses, sheep, and cows he can kill before we send him to the big doghouse in the sky?"

"Chump!" I muttered.

I was logging in to the chat rooms on-line less and less. For a while I'd seen opinions about Riley and sometimes offered mine. But now I never saw his name mentioned.

"The public is fickle," Grace pronounced.

I thought fickle was only about girls and dates and stuff like that, but Grace doesn't use the wrong word often, so I had to agree with her. The public is fickle. Now all the chat was about the plan for a new skate-board park where we have the putting green. There were a lot of different opinions on that one, too.

Now there were only eight spaces left on my calendar.

We called Joel Bell. "As I said," he told us, "nothing left to do but wait." He sounded sad and sympathetic, but that didn't seem enough to me.

"Aren't we paying you to do extra?" I asked in the tone of voice you don't use to adults and definitely not to a lawyer. But I was pretty desperate.

Mom, who was standing by the open refrigerator,

turned and gave me a horrified look.

Mr. Bell didn't sound horrified. "If there was more I could do, I'd do it, son. I know how you feel."

But how could he? Riley wasn't his dog.


Stephen started coming over for dinner more and more. "I can't resist your mom's home-cooked meals," he told me. "Usually I eat only frozen dinners or canned stuff."

I didn't look at Mom when he said that. And she didn't look at me. There's no doubt, Mom is the best disguiser of frozen meals in this or any other universe. Stouffer's should hire her. Campbell's, too.

"I saw Riley in the exercise yard today." Stephen helped himself to another chicken enchilada. "He gets along great with the other dogs."

I nodded. "He likes other dogs." I was remembering the time we met the lady with the little bitsy rat of a dog and how nice Riley had been. I was beginning to hate those kinds of memories. They made me sad.

"A couple of days back, I saw him wrestling with another dog over a chewed-up bunny toy they both wanted," Stephen said. "Riley got it, but then he walked away and gave it up."

"How come?" I asked.

"The other dog was a little Scottie. And a female." Stephen grinned at me. "I figured Riley let her have it because he's a gentleman."

"He is," I said. "He's a real gentleman."

I was always glad when Stephen came. He always had good stories about Riley to tell me. It made me feel better to know he wasn't just lying around moping.

The next time I saw Stephen, I had a new bunny toy for him to take to Riley. "Tell him I sent it," I said.

And then, when there were only five nights left, the most awful thing happened. I was lying in bed, listening to my Walkman, thinking about Riley, when he disappeared on me. I squeezed my eyes shut and pulled off the Walkman, concentrating. But I couldn't get Riley's exact face. It was just a dog blur, an anonymous everydog dog. It was like looking in a bathroom mirror that's steaming up and seeing your face get foggier and foggier.

My heart thumped. Where was Riley?

I grabbed my pillow and pressed it to my face, but his smell was so faint I could hardly get it. I turned on my lamp and slid out of bed and stood in front of the

big picture of him that I'd taped together; in an
instant he was back. How could I have forgotten?
Those ears, those big, soft eyes? There was no one to
see, so I kissed his face with the long torn scar all the
way down it and went back to bed. But I couldn't get
what had happened out of my mind. I suppose saving
him *had* become a kind of game against Ellis and
Duane and others, and I'd lost Riley in the need to
win it.

I thought about my grandpa and he was still
there, even to the way the little sprout of white hair
flicked up at the back of his head. I decided I'd con-
centrate on him every single night before I went to
sleep and keep him safe inside of me.

I hoped losing Riley that way didn't make me a
shallow person. From now on, I'd be careful to think
of him and not our war plans.

I was still freaked, so I got out of bed again and
went down the stairs. There was music playing in the
kitchen, and I stopped at my usual bend in the stairs.
Below, there was only the music. From the bend, I
can't see or be seen, but not seeing can be frustrating,
especially like now. I went silently down the two
extra steps that took me around the curve.

Our kitchen is big. I guess you could maybe even

call it a family room. It's certainly where we spend most of our time. The floor is made of big square flag-stones. There's a rug over by the table. The CD player and radio sit up on a dresser that holds Mom's teapot collection.

Tonight she and Stephen were playing a CD, one of those oldies that Mom likes. I didn't know the name of whatever it was, but Mom and Stephen were dancing to it. Some guy was singing, "Only you can make this world seem right." Mom's head was on Stephen's shoulder, and they were moving very slowly, dreamily almost.

I went back up the two steps and sat down in my hiding place. My chest hurt.

So, I'd seen them dancing, so what? Adults like to dance. But I'd seen more, and I wasn't sure exactly what. I'd seen one of those things you can't put a name to. Like maybe you could say closeness, or fondness. I didn't know. Maybe you could say love.

*Chapter 16*

Three days left.

The next day was the annual Monk's Hill Old-fashioned Summertime Picnic in Carlisle Park.

"What do you mean you're not coming?" Grace jumped out of her chair.

We were on the porch, sitting in the half-light. We'd been playing checkers till it got too dark and I'd beaten Grace five times straight. I'm a very good checkers player. My dad taught me. "It's because I think ahead," I've told Grace more than once. My dad taught me that, too.

Grace stood staring as I stacked the red and black checkers in their cigar box. "What do you mean you can't come?" she asked again.

I didn't look up. "I can't, that's all. Not when all the time I'll be thinking about what might happen on Monday."

"But, look! There's nothing more we can do. Honest, William. See? You're thinking ahead again and that's okay for checkers, but not when you can't plan or . . . or have a strategy. Our strategies are all used up."

I closed the lid of the cigar box and ran my hand over the faded picture on the lid—a girl with rosy cheeks and black curly hair with a cigar in her mouth—which I'd drawn in with Magic Marker when I was really little. The trees in our yard were filled with twittering birds. Moths circled the porch, banging themselves against the screen door in the oblong light.

Grace sat down again. "What does your mom say?"

"She says it would be good for me to get away. To have fun. She says it'll spoil it for you and for her if I don't go."

"It will," Grace said. "Who'll be my partner in the sack race? Not one of my nerdy little brothers, that's for sure. And Mitch Webster and His Insane Five are playing again."

"Stephen's going," I muttered.

"So? You mean he'll be my partner in the sack race? Give me a break. He'll be with your mom."

I hadn't told Grace what I'd seen from my hiding

place on the stairs: Mom and Stephen and the way they had their cheeks together as they danced. It was kind of personal and private. Had Mom and my dad ever danced like that?

"Let's get your mom out here and see what she thinks," Grace pleaded.

We could hear her inside, talking on the phone to my aunt Jo, who lives in Utah. They talk a lot. They exchange recipes because Aunt Jo is exactly the same kind of cook Mom is; they tell each other secret ways to make delicious vegetable soup by combining three cans and adding sour cream. . . . "This culinary artistry is part of our genes," Mom says.

"She's probably in the middle of an important recipe now," I told Grace. "And besides, you're just hoping for two against one. For the picnic . . ."

I stopped.

Peachie was coming up our driveway. She was wearing her long khaki shorts and a baggy blue-checked shirt that might have been Woodie's once, and she was carrying a humongous bunch of pink roses. I felt this drench of panic. Why was she coming over here?

"Oh, man," I whispered. "What now?"

Grace and I stood, waiting.

Peachie stopped at our pond, which was now just

a big dirty, dusty hole in the ground. I could hear this thump, thumping inside of me, like bongo drums. What if I dropped dead right now?

She was coming up the steps.

"Mom," I called, loud enough and hysterical enough to probably make her cut off from Aunt Jo without even saying good-bye. She pushed through the screen door just as Peachie got to the top step.

"I was just looking at Matthew's pond," Peachie said in the saddest voice imaginable. "I miss him."

Matthew is my grandpa . . . was.

"I know," Mom said. "You two were such good friends." She stepped forward to kiss Peachie's cheek then said, "Won't you sit? Here? Grace, can you fluff up the pillow?"

Grace did while I stood, stiff as a zombie.

Peachie held the roses out to Mom, who buried her face in them.

"Peachie. They're lovely. Thank you."

And then Peachie said, "Hello, William."

"Hello."

"Over here, Peachie." Grace patted the fluffed-up cushion invitingly.

"Thank you." She sat.

"May I get you some lemonade?" Mom asked, and Peachie shook her head.

"I'm only staying a minute. I came to tell you that I'm going to be gone for a while."

"Oh?" Mom sat on the edge of the glider, still holding the roses. "Gone where, Peachie?"

"To my sister's. She's hurt her back and she needs me. So the Sultan and I will head on up there for as long as is necessary." She looked at me. "William, I wanted you to know. And I want you to know that I will be back. This is my home and the Sultan's, and no one is going to drive us out."

"I don't want to drive you out, honest, I don't," I said too loudly.

Something skittered across the porch roof. A night bird, maybe.

Mom sat straight. "What do you mean 'drive you out,' Peachie?"

"Well, I'm afraid there are some people who would like to see me leave Monk's Hill," Peachie said.

"Not me," I said again. "I don't think you should leave."

I saw the glimmer of Peachie's smile. "Not you, William. I never thought it would be you."

"But what happened?" Grace was fanning herself with the folded-over checkerboard.

Peachie smoothed her hands over the legs of her shorts. "I've been getting e-mail. Several e-mails. None of them very nice. And phone calls. Two in the middle of the night. One man asked how I would like to have my horse put down. He said it didn't seem to bother me to have someone else's animal killed, just because I was angry at it."

"But how did they get your e-mail?" Grace asked.

Peachie smacked at a mosquito that had landed on her shirt. "I haven't been too careful about that, I'm afraid."

"And who would say such awful things?" Mom asked. "Who?"

Grace groaned. "Some of those guys who signed our petitions were pretty extreme."

"The other side, too," I put in quickly.

Peachie turned to face me. "Both sides, I'm sure."

I was still holding the cigar box. Peachie smiled. "Still beating everybody at checkers, William?"

I nodded. "Sometimes."

"Remember when you and I used to play? I wiped you out a couple of times, didn't I?"

I nodded again.

"You should know something before I go," Peachie said. "I wrote a letter to the commissioners. I told

them that since I now know your dog won't be coming back here, I'd like to withdraw my complaint."

"You did?" My heart leaped. "You did?"

Grace jumped up. "Peachie, you are an angel!"

"It didn't make any difference, William. Their
thinking is that a dog like that will do it again, wherever he's placed. He'd be put up for adoption. They'd
have to warn . . ." She stopped. "He'd be hard to
place. They said they'd take it under consideration."

"Oh, Peachie, Peachie, thank you," I said. "It's—
it gives me hope!"

"I was very angry when Riley came after my
horse." Peachie's voice was low and tight. "But time
passes. And anger cools. The Sultan is all right. But
it's been a hard time. He and I can both use a break.
And I'll be useful to my sis at the same time."

She stood. "I hope whatever happens, your dog is
allowed to live," she said to me.

Then to Mom, she said, "Maybe you'll call me at
Ellen's and let me know."

"I will. When are you leaving?"

"Tomorrow, early. I'm already packed up. And
one more thing. Will you keep an eye on my house?
I wouldn't want anything to happen to it . . . you
know . . . if some crazy knew I was gone . . ."

"At least come over before you go and let us fix you breakfast," Mom said.

"Thanks." Peachie smiled. "Thanks. But we'll just stop and get it on the way."

She hugged Mom and Grace and held out her hand to me. But then she and I were hugging, too. "I'm sorry you got all those mean e-mails," I whispered.

"I'm sorry about a lot of things. But sometimes you can't go back, no matter how much you want to."

Then she was gone, striding through the moon shadows that lay on our driveway, through the night scent of honeysuckle.

I felt this awful mixture of sorrow and guilt. "Well, she started it," I said halfheartedly.

Mom shook her head. "Not really."

Grace, looking exactly like a Halloween witch, hissed, "Why don't you clam up, William? What if she never comes home? What are you going to say then?"

Peachie had reached the gate now, and we watched as she disappeared into the dark beneath the trees.

# Chapter 17

I went to the picnic after all, wedged between Mom and Stephen in his truck. I'd decided I couldn't stay home, staring at all those dead, Xed-out days on my calendar, thinking of Riley, thinking of Peachie. Our kitchen was filled with the smell of her roses.

How could anybody scare her like that? Her all alone and really old and with only the Sultan to protect her? And she *was* scared. She'd just about admitted she was glad of an excuse to leave. What if she did leave forever? Then I could have Riley back. I felt guilty the minute the thought came to me.

I studied her house as we passed. Already it had that not-lived-in look, with the shades drawn and the barn door closed. A soft drizzle was falling, and the sky was gray and mournful.

"I was going to get up early to say good-bye,"

Mom told me. "I set the alarm. I thought about wak-ing you, too, William, and both of us going out to wave to her. But then, well, I didn't want to make it be like a final parting. You know, make too big a thing of it. She'll be back."

I nodded, staring straight ahead at the wipers going back and forth, fanning little wedges of clean glass on Stephen's dirty windshield. They squeaked out a little rhyme:

> *Going, going, gone.*
> *Everybody, everything*
> *Gone, gone, gone.*

I glanced up at Stephen. He was wearing an Oregon Ducks cap and his hair curled out around it.

"Are we going to have fun today, William?" he asked.

I shrugged. My eyes were blurred up, worse than the windows.

Carlisle Park looked sad. Wet dripped off the trees and beaded the tops of the picnic tables. The cars, double-parked all the way around the edges of the grassy field, were slick with rain. We could see the dark shapes of people inside them, waiting for the drizzle to stop.

Mom opened her door an inch, then closed it again. "It'll be over soon," she said. She leaned forward and pointed out the front window at a patch of blue. "Big as a pig's waistcoat, right, William?"

"Right." That was one of Dad's sayings that means if there is even that much blue, the rain will soon drift away.

It did. The blue widened, then widened more. And there was the sun. People streamed out of their cars and trucks like they were bears bursting out of their winter caves.

I'd spotted Grace's family station wagon earlier, on the other side of the park. Her two little brothers were first out, then Grace. I squeezed past Mom and flailed my arms. "Over here, Grace."

She came running across the field. "William!" she said breathlessly. "It's great you changed your mind about coming. Want to go sign up for the Frisbee competition?"

We signed up for everything, the way we do every year. The grass was damp, but not squelchy, and it didn't bother anybody. "Of course not," Mom said. "We're true Oregonians."

Grace and I ran in the sack race while the Insane Five blasted out some hot salsa music. In about three steps we tripped each other and fell together in a lumpy heap. "You're not supposed to take *strides*," Grace scolded. "You're supposed to hop, William. You're supposed to coordinate with me."

We wriggled out of the cold, wet sack. "How about you coordinating with me?" I scolded back.

"I swear, I would have done better with one of my dorky brothers," Grace grumbled.

"So don't be my partner next time," I said. Grace and I go through this every year.

It seemed half of Monk's Hill had come, never mind the rain. I saw Officer Zemach, who'd taken away Riley on that awful night.

She waved to me and called, "Good luck, William." I think she meant about Riley and not about the three-legged race coming up next.

Mr. Bingham, the photo shop man, asked if I'd heard anything yet and squeezed my shoulder.

Pete, who owns Pete's Hardware, said, "William? Are you still planning on finishing that pond? I'll take back that butyl liner, you know, if you've no use for it."

"Thanks," I said. "I'm not sure."

Pete nodded. "Just give me a call."

Ellis Porter and Duane Smith were sitting on one of the picnic tables. Each time someone fell, they cheered and whistled.

"Typical," Grace said. "Typical dweeb attitude."

The adults had their own sack race, and every kid watching turned into a dweeb, too. We catcalled and booed and blew raspberries as they fell. I watched Mom and Stephen. They toppled over quickly, laughing into each other's faces as they rolled on the wet grass, squirming free of their sack.

In the truck, on the way here, they hadn't given any hint of the way they'd been last night when they were dancing. There'd been no lovey-dovey looks or anything like that. They hadn't held hands. Of course, that would have been pretty hard with me sitting between them.

I made myself look away.

Riley would have loved this park, all the space, the trees. But even if we still had him, he couldn't have come today. Dogs are not invited to the Monk's Hill Old-fashioned Summertime Picnic. Those that were here were locked into cars with the windows cranked down just enough to tempt them with the day outside.

There was a mockingbird perched on a picnic bench. I played a game with myself. If it flew up into the oak tree, the commissioners would vote for Riley on Monday. If it flew up onto the wire, they'd vote against him. I clenched my fists in my pocket. Fly into the tree, bird. Go to the tree. It hopped onto the grass, darted low into the shrubbery, and disappeared. I told myself it was a stupid game anyway.

I took second place in the Frisbee-throwing competition and Grace took fifth. "Just a fluke," she told me. "I'm better than you any day." Grace, to use her own words, has superior self-esteem.

Throwing the Frisbee reminded me of Riley, of course. Everything reminded me of him. But still, I figured being here was probably way better than being alone at home.

We did the Bunny Hop all the way around the field, everybody together, even Ellis Porter and Duane Smith. The Insane Five played and sang some corny song that went "Run, rabbit, run, run, run."

Mom and Stephen were in front of us. The red ribbon that held her hair back had come loose, and Stephen pulled it all the way off. He lifted her hair from her neck and tied the ribbon back on. The way she turned to smile at him over her shoulder gave me some kind of pang. I thought his fingers brushed her cheek, but I wasn't sure. Did I want this? What about Dad? Of course, he had Phoebe now. What was it Mom had said? "Your dad and I parted for good reasons. And for those good reasons we won't be getting back together." What was it Peachie had said? "Sometimes you can't go back."

It was close to noon now.

Mom and Stephen and Grace's parents went across to the picnic table where we'd left our stuff. They called us over. "We're getting ready to eat," Mom said. "William, we forgot to bring the extra blanket from Stephen's truck. Will you run and get it?"

Grace's dad was taking hot dog packages from the freezer chest. "Can you corral your brothers, Gracie? They're over there in the Flying Dutchman circle."

I caught the keys Stephen threw to me and raced toward the cars to get the blanket. A white station wagon had parked itself beside us, and as I ran past, something scrabbled loud and hard at the back window. *Yip, yip, yip.* The yipping was so loud it made me leap backward, and I bumped my elbow on the jutting-out mirror of the truck.

There was a tempest raging inside the station

wagon, and the tiny barking was as ferocious as tiny barking could ever be. A little terrier was glaring out at me from the inch-wide crack in the rear window. The dog was so small and the window so high that it had to stand on the back of the driver's seat, sliding off every couple of seconds, scrambling up again. Its nose was button-sized, black, wet as licked licorice. Its little teeth were baby doll teeth. I couldn't help laughing.

"Whoa! Whoa!" I held my hands out in front of me as if I were surrendering. "You're awful tough for such a puny guy. Relax, will you? I'm not going to steal your car!"

I rubbed my elbow. "And I dropped the keys. See what you made me do?"

There was another faint sound coming from somewhere close. What was it? A kind of snuffling. Another dog, maybe in the next-door van?

I saw the shine of Stephen's keys in the dirt and bent to pick them up, and that was when I saw the feet in black cowboy boots, the thick legs in strained-tight jeans, and realized there was someone crouched behind the truck, almost beneath the hedge. Whoever it was had his arm across his face, and it was from under the arm that the strange snuffling sound came.

"What . . . ?" I began, and I took another step forward. Though I still couldn't see his face, I recognized Ellis Porter. For a terrible second I thought maybe he was lying in ambush to jump me. But there was no way. He was hunched over, crying or something.

He lowered his arm. His face was twisted like a little hurt kid's.

"Ellis," I stammered. "What are you doing?"

"Dog," he whispered.

"Dog?" I repeated and pointed at the station wagon. "You mean the little guy back there?"

He jammed his knuckles into his mouth, gnawing at them. I could see he was terrified. Could this be supercool, supermean, superscary Ellis Porter? I'd never seen him like this.

How could I be sorry for him? But for a minute I was.

"It's okay," I said, and before I could think about it, I got down and crawled under the hedge with him.

# Chapter 18

**W**ho would have believed that I would have been sitting under a dripping hedge with supercool, supermean, superscary Ellis Porter and that he would have been jabbering at me, nonstop?

"I don't tell . . . I don't say." His voice jerked in bursts and stops.

"Was it the little dog that . . . that . . ." I began. Impossible to say the words "that scared you" to this guy! Instead I said, "That surprised you? He can't get out, you know. He was just defending his family's . . . car."

"I wish I would never see another dog for the rest of my life." He sounded calmer now.

"Well, I know that," I said. "You sure didn't give my dog much of a break." I couldn't hold back. "If you hadn't brought your rotten old petition . . ."

Ellis touched the scar above his lip, the one that gave his mouth the strange lopsided twist that Grace called his Evil Ellis look. "A dog did this," he said. "I was three years old. They say a person can't remember that far back. But I can."

He wasn't looking at me, and I thought maybe he was talking to himself and had forgotten I was there. Maybe I could just slither away. Why had I crawled in here beside him anyway? I took a deep breath and inched a space between us.

"The dog was loose. He wasn't that big either." Ellis nodded toward the station wagon, where I could see the little terrier standing on sentry duty on the ledge of the back window. Ellis's jaw quivered. "He was about that size."

Oh, I didn't like this. I wished Mom had never sent me for the stupid blanket. I wished someone would come by to go to the restroom, which was not that far away on the other side of the hedge, and where Ellis had probably been headed. I secretly glanced around. There was no one in sight.

"The dog was tied up outside the market," he went on in that zombie voice. "My mom turned away for a second and I bent to pet him. My mom says our faces were just about level when he snapped. He held on. They couldn't make him let go."

I shivered. "That was bad, all right. But you know all dogs are not mean. Anyway, he was probably scared of you."

"That's what the doctors say, among other things." He blinked and suddenly focused on me. "My cat. I told you what happened to her. Three of them came after her. She didn't have a chance. And do you want to know the worst of it? The very worst of it?"

I wanted to say, "Not really," but I felt myself nod. It was as if I was mesmerized and Ellis was one of those hokey TV hypnotists.

"I saw those dogs coming. I saw them all the way down the street. I ran in the house and shut the door and watched from the window. I saw them drag Josephine off the top of the car. I saw every bit of it, but I was too scared to go out and save her. All I wanted to do was hide. Like now."

"Oh, man!" I muttered. I didn't know what to say or do. Should I reach out and touch him? But you couldn't reach out and touch Ellis Porter. He'd massacre you.

I pushed my fingers in and out of Stephen's key ring. There was a little metal dog dangling from it, and I palmed it in my hand.

"It would probably have been dangerous for you to go out," I said weakly.

Ellis wasn't listening. "I could have taken the broom. Or my baseball bat. I could have thrown something. Shouted."

It wasn't hard to tell he'd been through this in his head a million times. But why was he telling me? I edged away and stood up.

"I think you can learn not to be afraid," I said. "Like if you're afraid of flying, they take you into . . ."

"Shut up," Ellis said.

Someone was clumping between the cars, making the little terrier have another frenzy fit.

"Hi!" Grace skidded to a stop beside me. "What's keeping you, William? The hot dogs are ready." She stared at Ellis. "What's going on? Did you and William have another fight? Did William knock you down again?" She beamed at me.

"No," I said. "Here are the keys, Grace. Get the blanket."

Ellis scrambled up so fast I took a step backward, the way I'd done when the little dog yipped at me, bumping into Grace this time instead of the mirror.

"You breathe a word of this to anybody, Halston," he said to me, "and I'll knock your head off." He was definitely back to normal now. He glowered at Grace. "That goes for you, too, little girl."

"Little girl!" Grace looked ready to explode.

"You know what, Porter?" I spoke in a calm but masterful voice. "Getting rid of my dog isn't going to help you any. You never even knew him."

"Shut up about your mangy mongrel," Ellis said. "Do you think I care what happens to him? Far as I'm concerned, he'll just be one less . . ."

"You're not going to be able to forget what you let happen to your cat. Not ever. Josephine is going to haunt you, and if Riley doesn't . . . if Riley . . ." I swallowed. "If Riley isn't set free, then I hope he haunts you, too.

"C'mon, Grace," I said.

"That was way cool, William," she breathed. She half turned. "We forgot the blanket."

"Leave it," I said.

When I looked back, I saw Ellis going through the hedge, making a wide, wide circle around the station wagon and the tiny dog inside.

# Chapter 19

O f course I told Grace everything Ellis had said. After all, I hadn't promised him anything.

Grace was agog. "But why did he tell you? Especially the bit about how he could have saved Josephine?"

I shrugged. "I haven't a clue."

But Mom had some clues when I told her that night.

We were sitting at the kitchen table. She'd put the cupcakes that were left over from the picnic on the big yellow plate Peachie had given us once.

"It was because you were there, William," Mom said. "Ellis was all shook up. This fear and shame has been building up in him. He was going to burst if he didn't let it out." She peeled the ruffled paper off the bottom of a cupcake and put it on my plate. "And in a way I think he was trying to explain himself to you. He was saying, 'This is why I'm afraid of dogs. This is why I didn't try to save Josephine. This is why I hate Riley. I'm not as bad a guy as you think.' Poor kid," she added. "The world is full of dogs. Imagine how awful it must be for him."

I peered at the cupcake as if I'd never seen one in my life.

"Eat it, honey. It's good. Duncan Hines."

"I'm not hungry," I said.

"I know."

"I can tell you think I shouldn't have knocked Ellis down," I said. "But I had the utmost provocation."

Mom smiled. "I imagine that's what Grace said."

I nodded. "And it's true."

"I'm sure it is."

There was a silence between us, not an easy one.

"I don't suppose you'd like to come sit in my lap, the way you used to," Mom said, and I managed a small grin.

"I don't think so. But thanks."

Her hands were folded on the table and her face was so gentle as she looked at me that it made my throat hurt.

"I think I'll go to bed now," I croaked.

"Take the cupcake with you," Mom said, which showed how unnormal tonight was. A cupcake in bed after I'd brushed my teeth! Never before in the history of the world.

Sunday morning.

Dad came over to go to church with us. He'd called two or three times each week to ask if there was news of Riley. It was weird how Riley had made us talk to each other more. Not a word, though, about Phoebe. I guess he was waiting for the right opportunity and he didn't believe this was it. Once he told me he'd been in touch with Joel Bell.

"What does he think?" I asked.

The pause on the phone before Dad answered let me know what Joel Bell, our smart attorney, thought.

"He'd hoped they might have handed down a decision by now," Dad said reluctantly.

Did that mean they'd decide sooner if the news was good? And hang back if it was bad? Hard to tell somebody his dog was going to die. You'd want to put it off, wouldn't you?

We sat in our usual seat in church. The three of us, me between them, like in the car with Mom and

Stephen. Two different guys was all. So strange when you thought about it.

Ellis Porter was with his dad four pews in front. I was glad I couldn't see his face.

When it was time for silent prayers, I prayed really hard for Riley. I always imagine everyone's prayers going up to God at the same time, probably all of them asking for stuff. How can He pay attention? Usually I wait till everyone else is finished before I silently speak. I figure I have a better chance that way. But today I started right in, no time to waste.

Right after the offering plate was passed, Grace played a flute duet with Tracy Simpson. It was "How Great Thou Art." I only knew that because Grace had told me ahead of time. I could see her dorky little brothers giggling and squirming down in their seats with embarrassment. Her mom and dad looked really proud, though. I have to say I'm in awe of Grace's courage to perform in public because she plays so badly. But I suppose in church all is forgiven.

Once or twice I looked across at Peachie's empty pew. It seemed to me it was the emptiest pew in the whole church.

Dad stayed for lunch. He'd brought crusty bread,

the kind Cora Putnam had bopped me with, and cheese and tomatoes and avocados, and he helped me set the big wooden table under the apple tree. It was a sunny afternoon with birds singing and a little breeze that kept lifting our paper napkins off the table and blowing them around the yard. Nobody mentioned the ugly, gaping hole right there in front of the porch. Nobody looked at it.

Mom had fixed apricot lemonade the way she sometimes does, and she'd brought out the fancy glasses with the stems that we use only for special occasions. Easy to see she was trying hard to make everything nice, to help cheer me up.

"William?" Dad poured us all lemonade. "I have a friend called Phoebe. Her next-door neighbor's cat had four kittens. Phoebe was wondering if you'd like one. She says they're very cute."

I curled my feet around the legs of the wooden bench. First mention of Phoebe. But I hated this offer of a kitten.

"Is this supposed to be a substitute?" I asked. "Instead of Riley?"

Dad leaned across the table. "Definitely not. I'd told Phoebe how you always wanted a kitten, that's all."

"I always wanted a dog more," I said too loudly.

"I know that, son." Dad looked sad for me.

"You might like to think about the kitten," Mom said gently. "Sometime. Not today."

I poked at the slice of bread on my plate, making finger holes in it. "I'll think about it," I muttered. And then I added, "Tell Phoebe thanks." At least she hadn't suggested a cute puppy. Maybe she was okay. Maybe she wasn't such a disease after all.

As he was leaving, Dad said to Mom real softly, "I'll call tomorrow."

Tomorrow. Tomorrow. The end of the calendar. The end of the waiting.

He hugged me hard and whispered, "Keep your chin up, old man." Grace and I have noticed that sometimes when he's angry or upset, Dad gets more arrogant. He'd been very arrogant today.

I hugged him back when he hugged me. So maybe he wasn't all ours anymore. But he wasn't all the way gone from us either.

The day crawled by. Grace's family had gone to visit her grandmother in Medford.

"They want me to play my flute for her," Grace said gloomily. "And Tracy Simpson won't even be there to help me out."

So I didn't have Grace.

Aunt Jo had sent me the new Harry Potter book for my birthday, and usually reading it takes me away from everything into the world of Albus Dumbledore and Professor Flitwick. But today even the Hogwarts couldn't keep my mind from jumping backward and forward. If only . . . if only.

I turned on the computer and logged on to the Internet. As usual, it took a while. This time I tried searching with Yahoo. I typed in "dog."

*Digital Dog.*

*Dog Information.*

*Dog Chat.*

Thousands and thousands of dog entries.

*The Dog Within Us.*

*The Care and Feeding of Dogs.*

On and on I scrolled down the long list. If so many people loved dogs, why wouldn't they give me back mine?

I added "rescue," something I'd done before, but not on Yahoo.

*Old English Sheepdog Rescue of California.* I'd seen that one before on AOL.

"Riley's almost a sheepdog," I'd told them.

Almost wasn't enough.

*Swiss Search Dog Association.* I'd called them, too.

I'd called eleven different listings without any success.

"He's not the right breed, the right size, or in the right place," I'd told Grace angrily. "They're full. They have no more room. They have too many dogs already."

I switched off the computer.

Mom and I had dinner on the couch in front of the TV. We watched *True Grit,* an old TV movie that we'd both seen before. If John Wayne were here, he'd ride into that cage and rescue Riley, throw him over his saddle, and ride off with him into the sunset. But maybe not. John Wayne probably liked horses better than dogs, and he'd be on the Sultan's side.

The movie ended at ten after ten. No way to put off going to bed any longer.

I peeled the tape from the corners of the calendar without even X-ing in this, the last day, folded it small, and put it in the kitchen trash can. The end of the calendar. The end of the waiting. Now there was just tomorrow.

# Chapter 20

Riley was going to be euthanized. We got the call.

Euthanized is just another word for being put to sleep. Which is another word for being killed.

It wasn't Joel Bell who called at 10:30 in the morning to tell us. It was my dad.

When the phone rang, I rushed to it. As soon as I heard his voice, I gasped, "Dad, I can't talk now. We're waiting for Mr. Bell to call us."

"William?" The way he said it made my breath stop. I think I knew from that one word. "I asked Joel Bell to let me know so I would be the one to tell you," Dad said, ". . . good news or bad."

Mom was at the kitchen table, staring at me over the top of the *Monk's Hill Gazette.* The paper shook in her hands. She put it down and came to stand next to me.

I swallowed hard. "So . . . is it good or bad?"

"I'm afraid it isn't good, son."

Which was another way of saying it was bad. Another way of saying my dog was to be euthanized.

I stood there, my hand clenched on the phone, staring at the wall. It had an old piece of Scotch tape stuck on it where I'd once put up the list of numbers of my soccer team.

Mom unpried my fingers, took the phone, and asked Dad, "When?" Her back was turned to me as if to save me from knowing, but I already knew the worst, didn't I? "I think it's better to just tell him," she said. And then, "Thanks, Douglas." She hung the phone back on its hook, put her arm around my waist, and turned me toward her. I leaned my head against her instead of the wall.

"When?" My mouth felt numb as if I'd been to the dentist.

Her arm tightened around me. "Tomorrow."

I don't cry very often. I mean, I don't cry hard and out loud very often. I did when Grandpa died and maybe back when I was little. I cried now. I pulled myself away from Mom, went up to my room, and lay down on the bed with my face pressed into the pillow.

Downstairs, the phone rang and there was the murmur of Mom's voice. It rang again and again.

Sometimes it didn't ring, and I still heard the low sound of talking anyway. She'd be calling Aunt Jo to tell her. And Grandma and Grandpa Halston. And probably Peachie at her sister's house. Hadn't she promised to do that? She'd be calling Stephen. Of course, he might know already. At the pound they might have started getting things ready for the execution.

After a long time, Mom came upstairs. "Grace wants to know if she can come over."

"Not now," I said.

Mom nodded. I heard her go back down the stairs, her soft speaking-voice.

My mind jumbled around.

Was there anything else I could do? Anything? There was such a thing as a last-minute reprieve, wasn't there? I'd seen that in movies. The guy walking to the room where they had the electric chair, and the phone ringing and someone saying, "The governor has granted a stay . . ."

I pushed the pillow onto the floor and sat up. How come I'd never appealed to the governor? Who was he anyway? I couldn't even remember his name.

Mom knew and she helped me find his number.

"Sweetheart," she said, "I don't think it's going to do . . ."

I stopped her.

Someone was answering the phone. The governor was in Bermuda on vacation, I was told. His secretary did not feel it would be appropriate or beneficial "to interrupt him for this."

"I guess my dog's not important enough," I shouted, and Mom took the phone from me and said, "Shhh, William. Shouting doesn't help."

Neither she nor I wanted any lunch.

"Stephen says to tell you how sorry he is," she told me.

I shrugged. "Is he going to be the one to do it?"

Mom stared at me. "Do what?"

"Kill my dog."

"You know he wouldn't, couldn't, do that to Riley."

"Why not? That's part of his job, isn't it? Killing dogs?"

Mom spread her hands. "I don't know," she said miserably.

"It doesn't matter who does it." I slumped into one of the chairs.

Later I went outside and walked around our yard, round and round. I went into Peachie's yard, past the Sultan's closed stable door. I'd seen Mom water Peachie's roses a couple of days back, but I took the hose and watered them again, and watered the fuchsia and the hedges that were twined with honeysuckle and sticky blue flowers. The stream of water was a ribbon of diamonds, looping toward the sun.

The drapes in the living room weren't tightly closed, and when I peered through the gap, I was looking at the painting of the Sultan on the wall above the couch. Peachie wasn't gone forever. She'd said she'd be back and she would never leave that painting behind. She'd be back, she and her horse, and there'd be no big galumphing dog around to bother either of them. Riley was the one who'd be gone forever.

I went back to my house and upstairs to Grandpa's room. I brushed my hair with his hairbrushes and watched myself in his mirror. I was as numb as a rock.

I went to the kitchen and sat in front of the computer. The message came across the screen: *Unable to connect to server.* Stupid server. Always busy.

I waited and tried the Internet again. This time it came up.

All the same old dog listings. Nothing different.

*Buddy the Dog Hero*. I'd already read about him.

*Terriers Who Tried*. Tried what? I couldn't remember.

And then . . . and then. Every muscle I had pulled as tight as a rubber band. What was this? I hadn't seen this before. Something new. My eyes darted across the printed words without understanding the sense of them. I made myself read them out loud, taking the words into my brain.

"Mom!" I screamed. "Mom. Come here. You're not going to believe what I've found. Come here and see this."

I wasn't going to send an e-mail. I needed to talk, one-on-one. Information gave us the number.

"I'll pay for the call," I whispered as I waited for it to ring on the other side. "I've got money left."

Mom was smiling. "Don't worry. We have loads of money. Your dad's paying for the attorney . . ."

I interrupted. "But a call to Texas . . . must cost . . ."

"Don't worry," she said again, and stopped talking as I held up my hand.

"Hello? Are you Rudi Corona?" I asked.

"No, but I'll get him."

I held on. Someone was shouting, "Rudi! Phone call!"

Mom squeezed my hand. "I'm praying," she whispered.

I shuffled my feet. Impossible to stay still.

"Rudi Corona," the voice on the phone said.

"Hi." My heart drummed against my ribs. "My name is William Halston, from Monk's Hill, Oregon. I wanted to ask you . . . to tell you . . ."

He only interrupted me once. "What sort of a law is *that?*" he asked. "You're saying he has to be killed simply for chasing a horse? Not even attacking him?"

I nodded, then realized he couldn't see me. "That's all. My friend Grace calls it a putrid law."

"I'll say."

I truly thought his voice sounded just like John Wayne's. I pictured him in a cowboy hat.

The whole story of the flyers and the posters and the advertisements spilled out of me, and in the end, I said, "Please, please can you take him? It's his only chance."

"Sounds like you tried real hard, William. But

your dog's not a Border collie, is he? So far that's all I've used."

"No," I said. "He's part collie, though. That's what Stephen, he's sort of the vet at the pound, says. The rest of him is Lab. He's really fast, though. He can go like the wind. Running is his favorite thing." Sobs were coming and I couldn't stop them.

There was this awful silence when I could just about hear Rudi Corona considering, wondering if he should take a chance, or maybe wondering how to say no in a nice way.

"What do your parents say about this proposition?" he asked at last.

"My mom, she thinks it would be great. My dad's not here, but I know he would, too. He wants my dog to live and for me to be happy."

Vaguely, through all the muddle in my head, I heard what I'd said and I knew it was true. That's what Dad did want.

"And don't worry about expenses," I said quickly. "I've got money, and if there's not enough, my mom and dad will help." I was shaking so much I didn't think I could push out any more words, but I did. "Please save my dog."

"Take it easy, son." His voice was so soft I could

hardly hear. "Let me speak to your mom."

I handed over the phone and watched her, listening. "We'd be willing to do all that," she said. "We'll be waiting. I can't tell you what this would mean to my son." After a pause, she said, "Yes, I expect you do understand."

When she hung up the phone, she touched my cheek. "He's calling the commissioners right now. But William, if he does get permission to take Riley, well, it may not work out. It may end up that Mr. Corona can't use him in Texas after all. And then . . ."

I pressed my hands tight against my ears. I didn't want to think about it not working out. It had to.

# Chapter 21

Riley was going to go to Abilene, Texas, to learn how to be an airport dog. He was going to be trained to wait, along with other dogs, on the edge of the big private airport field. At Rudi Corona's command, he'd race across the grass and chase the birds that were massed there. They'd rise into the sky, and then the runways would be clear and safe for the small jets to take off.

The words I read on the screen were: "These Border collies are not for the birds.

"Birds get sucked into jet engines and the propellers of small planes. Even one bird can cause an accident. Airport owners have tried everything to discourage birds from congregating on runways. Finally they discovered that dogs are the best solution. They scare the birds away and save lives, the lives of people and the lives of birds." I'd just about stopped breathing.

Rudi called and told us what happened when he'd talked to the commissioners about Riley.

"If you're willing to try with this animal, we have no objections," they'd told him. "We have no desire to kill a dog that can be useful. But Texas is a long way from Oregon. Have we your assurance there will be no cost to the taxpayers?"

"None," Rudi Corona told them.

"And it will be a one-way ticket?"

"One-way," Rudi said. "All expenses paid for by the boy himself."

"And if the dog is not trainable?"

"I haven't met one yet that wasn't," Rudi said. "Dogs and I bark the same language."

So my dog was going to live. Not with me. But he was going to live. I'd told Mom, way back, that was all I wanted. And that's what I told myself again.

We had his one-way ticket to Texas. Counter-to-counter, it's called.

Stephen brought him to the airport in a big plastic carrier. It had a wire gate in front and a ventilation screen in the back.

"He'll be in the baggage compartment," Stephen told us earlier. "It's pressurized, so he'll be fine. It's too bad that from that far back he won't be able to see the movie, but heck! You can't have everything."

Mom and I and Grace went to the airport to see Riley off. I was filled with so many feelings. Excitement and longing to see him. Sadness at the thought that he was leaving us forever. Relief that this was the day he was to die, and he wasn't. Mostly I was dazed, the changes came so fast.

When Stephen's truck pulled into the parking lot, my insides were turning over so much I thought I might be sick. I could see the kennel, like a small red barn, in the back.

Stephen got out and called, "William? Help me lift this out. Your dog is no lightweight."

Mom gave me a gentle push to make my feet move, and I went across, peered through the criss-cross wires of the gate, and saw Riley. He looked back at me. He knew me. He made these little excited sounds. His tail swept across the kennel, thumping each side.

"We need to check him through pretty quick. Still . . ." Stephen scratched his head under his cap, checked his watch. "I'll just go talk to your mom and

Gracie for a minute. You stay with your dog."

Nice Stephen.

When I put my face against the mesh, Riley's big rough tongue came out, curled like a dry leaf so it would fit through the wire. It covered me with kisses. He licked at the salty tears that trickled down my cheeks. He wasn't making happy sounds anymore, and we stood in silence.

"You listen to what Mr. Corona teaches you," I whispered. "You're smart, Riley. It's going to be so great for you, chasing birds, being with other dogs."

I had brought some of his favorite Puppy Treat biscuits, and one by one I pushed them into the carrier. But he ignored them.

"Here's something else." I took his chewed-up, bald, stained tennis ball from my pocket. It wouldn't go through, of course, so quick, quick, before Riley knew what was happening, I unlatched the gate, dropped the ball inside, and closed it again fast. It fell in front of him. He nosed it, then looked at me. I think he was remembering the dog days when I tossed it for him in the yard, the way it rolled, the way we'd both chase after it and wrestle and tumble together in the silky weeds and grass. I think he was remembering. I longed to open the gate again and hug him, but I didn't dare.

I heard Stephen coming then, and I said, "Good-bye, Riley." That's what I tried to say.

Stephen touched my shoulder. "Time to get him on board, William. Grace and your mom have gone to find a baggage guy with a cart."

When they came back, we helped the baggage man lift the carrier onto a cart that was like a chunky little truck. He drove it toward the terminal and we hurried along behind.

Riley was parked by the counter. Lots of people stopped and admired him and asked where he was going and things like that. I looked straight ahead through the window, at the big jet that was waiting by the gate.

Grace said, "I bet he'll be the best dog Mr. Corona has. He'll be totally unsurpassed."

I nodded.

Mom gave the counter man Riley's papers that show he'd had his shots, and she filled in the forms that tell who was dropping him off and who was picking him up.

I looked around then and I saw Dad, shouldering through the people waiting to check in. "Traffic jam on the freeway," he muttered and came straight to

me, sliding a hand between the back of my collar and
my neck. I remembered when he used to always do
that.

"You were nice to come," Mom told him. "It's a
long drive from where you are."

Dad shrugged.

The luggage guy asked the ticket guy, "All set?"
and when he nodded, he said, "Off we go, then, pup.
Are you all traveling with him?" he asked us.

"No," Mom said. She held my arm and Dad stood
real close. Grace was crying. They all started mutter-
ing, "Good-bye, Riley. Good luck." Things like that.
Everyone sounded weepy.

I didn't say anything because Riley and I said our
good-byes already.

We stood, the five of us, in a sad little huddle,
watching as Riley was driven away.

## Chapter 22

We were eating supper when Rudi Corona called to tell us Riley had arrived. "Is he okay?" I tried to make my voice sound ordinary, but it was hard.

"He's more than okay. This dog has some appetite."

I smiled, remembering.

"I'll be in touch to let you know how he's doing," he said, and I thanked him.

We got an e-mail later that week. "He's learning fast. And he gets along well with the other dogs."

"He's not going to be sent back," I told Mom, and that was wonderful, of course. But it hurt, too. Riley was over for me. And when something's over, it hardly ever comes again. You just have to go along with it.

Summer was almost over, too. In my mind I called

it the summer of Riley because he had filled it up. In less than a week, it would be Labor Day, and soon after that, school would start. I wouldn't see Ellis or Duane in school, of course. But for sure I'd see them in town. Ellis might be embarrassed and leave me alone. Or he might be meaner than ever. With Ellis Porter, there's no way to tell. And that was something else I wasn't looking forward to.

"I've been thinking," Mom said the next morning. "Let's have a Labor Day party. We've had such a mixed-up summer. But now we've got something to celebrate."

"Good. Maybe Grace will play the flute." I stuck my finger in my throat and pretended to barf.

"We'll have to spruce up the yard," Mom said. "The serving table can go on the porch and small tables on the grass. Let's hope it doesn't rain."

I looked out of the kitchen window at the porch. One side of it was totally taken up by the giant roll of butyl liner. I looked beyond it at the hole in the grass that would never be anything but a hole. Our fishpond was over, too. And I had to accept that. But knowing that I had to didn't mean that I'd be forgetting Grandpa, did it? I never, ever would. Just like accepting that Riley was gone didn't mean I'd forget him.

"I'll call Pete's Hardware," I told Mom. "Pete said he'd come for that butyl liner anytime. That'll free up the porch." I paused. "Do you think Dad would help me fill up the hole?"

Mom's voice was soft. "You know he would."

But in the end it was Stephen who helped me because Dad had gone to Colorado to spend the holiday with Phoebe and her parents. But Stephen was okay. Already I knew he was going to be a part of our family . . . not a dad to me exactly, because I still had a dad. But a good friend. And that was okay, too.

The party was a blast. A detonation, Grace called it. Tons of our friends and neighbors came, and they seemed really glad about the new news of Riley.

There was no Peachie. No Sultan to look curiously over the fence, pushing out his head to have his nose petted, scarfing little secret forbidden treats.

Things wouldn't be the same when they came back because so much had changed. But I could work on it. I knew Peachie would want to, too.

When the party was over and Mom was saying

good-bye to Stephen out at his truck, I sat by myself at the kitchen table. The refrigerator looked bare with no red X–marked calendar. I slid my feet back and forth across the rug where Riley used to lie. Nothing else of him here except memories. He was gone.

Mom had made tea for her and Stephen. I picked up her cup, tipped it over on its saucer, and turned it three times in the way that makes the leaves settle just right.

I peered inside and instantly saw a dog running, ears back, tongue lolling. "Riley," I whispered. *"You're happy.* You're totally unsurpassed. The tea leaves never lie."

I felt free and happy myself.

No matter that Mom says you see only what you want to see in the tea leaves. No way! I peered into the cup again and smiled.

I believe.